ENDORSEMENTS

"In this spellbinding tale where fiction becomes reality, a struggling author must wield her pen to save a magical world she unknowingly brought to life, blending creativity with high-stakes adventure in a thrilling race against time."

~ NewInBooks.com

"This book was breathtakingly beautiful."

~ KasFire Reviews

"Avery Sage has an amazing talent for writing speculative fiction. Engaging and full of suspense, her work keeps me on the edge of my seat... from the first paragraph, I found myself unable to put down the story until the very last word."

~ Dana Kendall, Amazon Best-selling Author

"The author writes an action packed story that will keep you on the edge of your seat trying to read faster and turn the pages faster to see what is going to happen next."

~ Goodreads

book
one
Seeing
is not
Believing

BOOKS BY AVERY

~ CALL OF THE SEA ~
Siren's Charm
Mermaid's Kiss
COMING SOON

~ DESPERATE MEASURES ~
Seeing is not Believing
Knowing is not Saving
COMING SOON

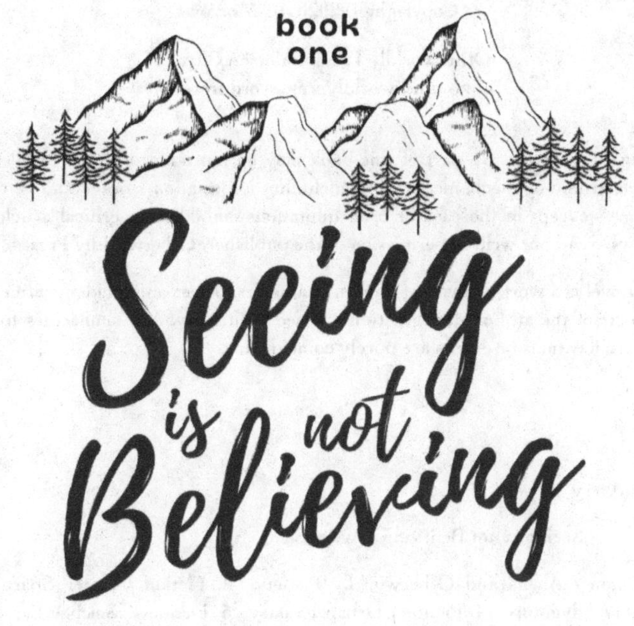

Seeing is not Believing

Avery Sage

Sage, Avery

    Seeing is not Believing / Avery Sage

1. Fiction / Aliens and Otherworldly Planets. 2. Fiction / Outer Space. 3. Fiction / Adventure. 4. Fiction / Urban Fantasy. 5. Fiction / Science Fiction & Fantasy / Supernatural. 6. Fiction / Science Fiction & Fantasy 7. Fiction / LGBTQIA+

ISBN: 978-1948733427 HARDBOUND
ISBN: 978-1948733441 PAPERBACK

Second Edition 2025

Printed and bound in the United States of America

for all of the people who believe,

even without a shred of evidence existing

that backs up that belief . . .

book
one
Seeing
is not
Believing

chapter one

Have you ever had one of those moments? One when you were absolutely certain you saw someone in the corner of your vision. But you knew it was impossible to have seen anyone—because no one else is there in the house with you!

When you live alone, and you're the type of person who tends to stay up writing late into the night, those moments can be more than a little frightening.

What would you do in that situation?

What would you do if one of those moments happened... and it wasn't even a little frightful? How would you handle it, if it was amazing... fantastic... unbelievable... even life-changing?

I can tell you what I did—not in one, but two cases.

The first time it happened, there was nothing particularly spectacular about it...

I shrugged my shoulders, took a deep breath, and dove back into the story that had kept me from sleep for so many days that I had finally lost count.

It was the latest in a long line of stories that had whispered to me urgently, keeping me distracted, until I worked feverishly to record every single bit of it.

Writing was much more than a passion for me. I had spent most of my life pursuing it... much like a starving man searches for his next meal.

First, moving across the country to attend college. I

eagerly plunged into my classes, studying literature and creative writing in all its forms, as well as a few other courses that piqued my interest. I focused mostly on classes that would enhance my writing.

I didn't bother to take physical fitness courses, since I waited tables until the early hours. Sometimes as much as seven nights a week.

I had found a tiny apartment to share with friends. And I continued to save every penny, carving out time to write when I should have been sleeping and turning down invitations from friends to party or socialize.

Whether or not exhaustion consumed my body when I stumbled in from work, the words came before everything else, including food, sleep, even chatting with my roommates.

After a quick shower, I would start a pot of coffee, pour a cup... and usually forget to drink it because I had lost myself in my writing. Eventually I would reheat it in the microwave, then I would promptly forget it again under the harsh taskmaster that was my own imagination.

And so it was, when I found myself aware of a presence occupying the same space as I, by way of a tell-tale shadow hovering at the corner of my vision during a time when I knew not one of my room-mates was at home. I stopped, sat straight up, and turned my head to where the person should have been.

Of course, there was nothing and no one there. No roommate creeping in to watch me work. No apparition or ghostly figure there to haunt me. No tell-tale shadow.

Whether or not it had been real or my imagination was the only question... one that had never truly been answered.

With no answers, and no hope of any, I had dived back into my writing, pushing the odd occurrence to the same corner of my mind where I held my own personal theories about fantasy, science fiction, and all of the beloved stories that had kept me company while growing up.

Nothing like that happened again. Not for many years. When it did happen again, I was writing in much the same circumstances, in the early hours of morning, as had become my habit.

I was alone in the house, this time due to a lack of roommates. I was again in the middle of a sentence. And ironically enough, I was working within the same story world.

Having sold my first story... one within what had been my favorite fantasy world for — at the time — a large sum, with no agreement for royalties or further earnings, and with no expectation of being allowed to write any sequels, I should have, by all rights, let the the story go.

But for some unexplainable reason I had never been able to. It had not been the first story I'd ever written, but there had always been something about it which had kept hold of me.

The characters and their world had stayed with me, so vividly that I'd written enough material to fill at least three full-length novels in the years since. This was in spite of three books from a completely different series that I had written and which had been published since.

So once again, I found myself sitting straight up in my chair, stretching muscles and bones too long cramped into the typical writer's hunch, and looking over at the deep armchair that rested beside the wide bay window that I loved so much, it had all but sold the house... a blessing for the harried, frustrated realtor who had shown me at least three dozen houses before this one.

In that favorite, overstuffed armchair, which I found such a wonderful place to curl up with a favorite novel the few times I tore myself away from my own writing, sat a man... a slightly strange looking man.

His eyes were too large for his face. His mouth had an oddly stretched look to it. His fingers were decidedly too long. His posture was much too still. And he looked at me in a way that felt more like he were looking through me, right into my head... my thoughts... or even beyond.

Though there was not one thing about the man, who was most certainly not human, that frightened or even startled me. His presence gave the impression of such respect and awe, that I could not help but feel as I did at one of the many events I had attended over the years.

These were events where I was asked to speak to readers, as well as to sign books, both from the beloved series that was well beyond my control and the unrelated ones that had, nevertheless, done exceptionally well all on their own.

Whenever I looked out on the crowds of people waiting to hear me speak, or standing in line with books clutched lovingly to their chests, or opened as they began to read —unable to wait even for the coveted signature before diving in, I felt the same sort of expectation that was flowing from the unearthly man calmly sitting in my favorite chair.

And in that moment, I knew... I absolutely knew... that whatever he was doing here, he meant me no harm.

Of course I had no way of knowing what he was doing here in my home, in a world that was clearly not his own. I would have thought I was dreaming, but for the pain in my neck from having it turned so far to look at him. For what was now turning into a very large amount of time.

With the pain demanding much of my attention, I determined to do something about it before trying to attempt an inquiry of this visitor. With deliberately slow movements, I unfolded the legs that were nearly asleep at any rate, and settled them to the floor in front of my computer chair.

Then I gently pushed against the wood until my chair began to roll backward, giving myself just enough room to allow the passage of my knees around the sides of the opening under my desk.

I nearly cringed as the wheels on the chair squeaked, but the man made no move, said nothing, did not even blink as my chair continued to roll.

I carefully moved my feet to swivel, turning my head slowly as I did so, determined to keep my eyes trained on the chair on the other side of the room and its occupant, certain that if I were to lose sight of him for even a moment, he would disappear as quickly as he had arrived.

He remained there. Whether it was because I kept my eyes on him or not, it was unclear. After several long moments, he finally moved, shifting forward so quickly, the movement itself was a blur. But there was nothing frightening in the movement.

On the contrary, I was fascinated, even if a bit confused at first. One moment he was sitting stiff and straight, and in the next moment he had shifted so that he perched on the edge of the large chair.

And still he said nothing.

I waited. Part of me wanted to speak, but again, I was hesitant that he would disappear if I spoke. I also felt there was a distinct possibility he did not speak my language. Though, why would he be here if he could not speak to me?

Seconds dragged out as I waited... stretched out until each one felt more like a year than a moment. I took the opportunity to look more closely at the strange being perched delicately on my chair.

His strange eyes were not only too large, they were inexplicably dark. There was no white area to be seen... just a grayish black that seemed to move and shift like the fog it so closely resembled.

It was impossible, no matter how I tried from this distance, to tell if his mouth was actually made up of two lips or not. There was a definite shape to the area of his face where humans had lips, but since he had barely moved — and had not yet spoken, there was no way to tell if it was actually his mouth, and whether that mouth was made up of lips or of something else.

His fingers, one of which had, at the moment I happened to look down at it, suddenly and inexplicably began tapping the arm of the chair where it rested in a complex sort of pattern.

There was no sound, just a constant movement that could have been anything... from the beat of a song that was stuck in his head... to some complex form of morse code that I could never hope to decipher.

I had but a moment to think what a disaster this would all turn out to be if that were the case, before he opened that strange mouth and spoke. And when he did, his voice so mesmerized me, that I very nearly missed the actual words he was speaking.

In fact, he may have actually repeated himself without my having noticed, so entranced was I by the sound of his other-worldly voice.

"We are in desperate need of your help." were the words I heard.

However, there was a distinct separation of sounds. What I heard spoken aloud was decidedly not English.

But those words—while clearly English—sounded as well, whether aloud or in my head, I could not tell.

Several long seconds passed again as I sat there, thinking about the sounds I'd heard, the entrancing sound of his voice, and the shape of his strange mouth as it formed the words.

Even as he was speaking unintelligible words, I marveled over the two distinct sets of words spoken and heard... or perhaps one spoken and one somehow magically translated only inside my head.

And then those strange lips widened in the most breathtaking smile I ever remember seeing in my life. Nearly terrible in its perfection, the smile lit up his entire face, making it almost painful to look at. I finally did look away... almost not caring whether he disappeared, yet at the same time terrified he would be gone when... if... I dared to look back.

Thankfully he did not disappear. After what felt like an eternity, I did look back. He was still in exactly the same position he'd been in, perched on the edge of my chair, no longer smiling now, but wearing an expression that was— for the first time—nearly frightening.

Before I could take it in that indeed I should be frightened, I heard the strange double layer of speech again, but this time with a compelling urgency that I seemed to actually feel deep within me as he spoke.

"Time is of the essence."

I managed to respond. "What does that mean, exactly? And how could I possibly help you? For that matter, who are you?"

"We are the link. We bring inspiration. We bridge the gap between worlds." He hesitated for a moment, while watching me. Perhaps to give me time to digest what had been said.

None of it really answered my questions, but clearly it was meant to do so. I nodded, but said nothing. Fortunately, he went on.

"Your world is unique in the vast cosmos we all inhabit. You wield a particular sort of magic, a tremendous force that fuels those in need." And once again, he waited.

I closed my eyes for a moment, taking time to think about what he had said. Had this strange visitor actually just told me that our world had magic... real magic?

Somehow I knew he didn't mean the type of magic one could see at an act in Vegas.

Was this supposed to be the way he wanted me to help them? Did he think I had magic? And that it was extremely powerful?

As I continued to try and make sense of his words — and the meaning behind them — he spoke again.

"You do not understand. This is expected." There was a tiny nod of his head, and then he kept going. "This is not the way our interaction is meant to be. Your people were never meant to know that we exist. We were to stay hidden, acting as your muse, providing inspiration only. This is the way of things." He stopped again, looking somewhat expectant.

And then, somehow, suddenly I was reminded again of that strange early morning so many long years ago, when I had been so certain someone was in the room with me. Only, when I had turned that morning to look, there had been no one in sight.

Had he been here then, too? Sitting in the same sort of place, because I'd had a chair in roughly the same place in my tiny room in that cramped apartment. A chair for the same purpose. A quiet place by the window where I could sit and read.

That time, when I had felt the hairs on the back of my neck stand up, feeling certain someone else was in the room with me — even though I had known it was impossible — I had looked for someone.

Had he momentarily forgotten to hide himself then? Or had he nearly shown himself for some other reason, only to change his mind and remain hidden before I had actually seen him?

He was nodding again in short, quick, blurred movements.

"You are correct."

That was it. Nothing else. No clues as to which part of the whole thing I was right about... which had me wondering if he could read my mind... or not?

He did not answer that question. He said nothing else, but continued to watch me for the moment. After several long seconds, I gathered up the courage to speak, voicing the question he hadn't answered, almost hoping he would answer with a yes—and at the same time, not really sure I wanted to know.

"Can you read my mind."

Before I had even finished asking, he was shaking his head. "We do not interfere in that way. We would not. We are only meant to inspire. We do not invade."

I realized, even as the words translated themselves somehow, he was still only half answering my query. Was he trying to answer, but was unable to accurately address every little bit, or was he deliberately answering only the part I must know? There was really no way of knowing, so it would have to do.

And now I felt certain that getting any answers would be much more difficult. Clearly there was some sort of language barrier here, even if it was only that his language did not seem to translate precisely into English.

I would have to be very careful—and very precise—if I hoped to understand the slightest idea of what exactly it was he thought I could do to help him... or them... or whatever.

Direct approach then... "All right. So, what exactly is it you need from me?"

He did not speak. He simply closed those large, strange eyes. A moment later, I pushed backward into my chair, nearly knocking it over.

Images were filling my head. Scenes I was familiar with. Scenes I had thought of all too often as I sat in my chair, writing—and wishing—that I could somehow visit the place I saw in my imagination.

There was the spectacular silver city I had written so much about. The waterfalls that thundered behind it were just as majestic as I had always imagined them. The sweeping green and blue fields that spread out on either side until meeting up with the dozens of industrial little villages that dotted the countryside around what I had always thought of as the capital city. The towering trees that sheltered those villages, and served as a comforting, familiar background.

There were people everywhere. A small group of children were running across the fields, trailing some kite-like sort of contraption. Several adults pushed heavily laden carts up the wide street that led to the main gates of the city. Others were tiny specks as they worked the distant fields of some blue-colored plant that I figured must be their version of wheat.

The clear, deep purple sky was dotted with fluffy silver clouds... comforting, reassuring, constant, cheerful.

It was the place of my dreams — of my fantasies.

chapter two

And then it wasn't.

There was no warning, no blink, no clue whatsoever that everything was about to change.

Oh, but change it did. Suddenly the cheerful sky was dark, threatening—the clouds menacing. There were no people to be seen, no children playing, no more industrious sights, no crops waving in a gentle breeze, no long expanse of grass.

And no trees that I could see.

The forest had been razed. Though there was no smoke, my imagination could easily see it spiraling up from where so many beautiful trees had been only a moment ago. The villages were mostly decimated as well. Only a few buildings remained that I could see, many of them obviously damaged.

And the city... the ruins of the once breath-taking city had tears springing to my eyes. I would have wiped them away, but the images were not blurred or washed away by them. So I allowed them to fall freely.

Where there had once been a magnificent city of silver towers and strong walls—buildings of such delicate artistry, I could scarcely believe I had actually imagined them—there was now a twisted heap of ruins and scrap.

Not even one tiny piece of the city remained intact. Every building had been destroyed. Every tower felled. Not one length of the wall that had once guarded that beloved city stood strong and true.

It was almost more than I could bear.

When I looked back to where the stranger was sitting— my eyes still full of tears—the images faded slightly, but remained in the distance of my vision. A shadow that would haunt me for a long time to come.

I tried to speak, to ask what this was supposed to mean,

but the words would not come.

Was this something he expected me to write about? Did he really think that my writing some horrific chain of events that would lead to this disastrous end for my beloved fantasy world could somehow help?

I sat there, my hands held up in a silent plea for someone... anyone... to tell me that the images I was seeing were not... could not... actually be real.

But that reassurance did not come.

After several long minutes of me trying to get my mouth to communicate something of what was rushing around in my head, I finally began to see that somehow, this was what he had been trying to tell me.

This strange being, although I could not imagine how, was showing me something that existed some place else. Very likely a place other than in our own galaxy, but somewhere out there... in perhaps another galaxy—or another dimension.

And he was asking me to do something to help them.

If he was asking me to write about this horrible place, to even begin to write of such atrocities as must have occurred to lead to such devastation, I didn't think I could bring myself to do so—especially not to the fantasy world I loved so much.

To the only true story of my heart, the one I had wished so many times I had somehow managed to keep a better control over, I could never destroy it in such a way.

I hadn't been exactly desperate, but I had been too quick in my naivety to accept terms that I knew now were near criminal, though I would never actually utter that statement aloud. There was still a tiny chance I would be allowed to publish one of the other stories I had written in that vast fantasy story world.

Or so the publisher and my agent kept telling me.

And now this stranger was here, showing me such disturbing images of my beloved Macus—as though the images were real.

With that thought, I gritted my teeth. I might not want to know, but I had to. I had to know if they were real. I had to know if some of them were real... or all of them. And I had to know if there was anything I could do to stop whoever or whatever was destroying my beloved fantasy world.

"These images..." I didn't get to even finish the question.

"They are real, Aura. You know this to be true. You have seen images of them before." He stopped a moment and I nodded.

The first ones he'd shown me. I had known they were familiar. I had seen all of them in my mind as I wrote about them. But I had managed to convince myself that I had dreamed them all up. Before I could ask again, he went on.

"The ones that are not known to you..." He sounded almost sad, which was somewhat reassuring to me. At least he was not happy about the sad state our beloved world—it was quickly becoming obvious that he cared for this world as I did—was in. When I nodded again, he continued.

"Those images are happening now. At this time. This is why I have come."

I sat a little straighter then. This was why he was here, then. So, maybe there was something that could be done.

"I believe you are the only one who can help us. Help them. Your writing is the key."

I must have looked puzzled because he stopped a moment, and then went on again, but I got the distinct impression that he changed what he was about to say, to answer my confusion.

"You do not understand. Forgive, please. I forget that you do not know." He made a gesture that made it seem as if he took a deep breath, but he made no movement to actually inhale air—and in that moment I realized he had not breathed visibly since he had arrived. It bothered me a bit, but I pushed it away. For the moment I was more concerned with the forthcoming explanation than with his strangeness.

"I am unable to tell you everything. I am able to tell you what I have already said. We come. We whisper inspiration to those like you." He did that quick, blurry nod when he could see that I remembered that he'd already said that.

"You write story. Humans read story. Magic is made. World is fed magic. World thrives."

I held up a hand to stop him. "Wait. So, are you saying that my story is somehow keeping this fantasy world alive? A world that I did not make up, but is in fact a real place somewhere out there?"

Another quick, blurry nod answered me, and I quickly went on.

"And you are also saying that there are other humans

writing stories, that are... what? Supporting other worlds that exist somewhere else?"

"You begin to understand." He sounded like a pleased teacher, speaking to a very slow child. I should have been insulted, but the very concept of what he was saying — what it all meant — was beginning to make me dizzy in its' perplexing hugeness. So I answered him in kind.

"Yes, I begin to understand."

He waited, most likely either seeing that I was dealing with quite a lot just now — or else he was reading my mind and knew how overwhelmed I was by all of this.

As I sat there thinking, I began to see the full extent of what he was telling me — and what those last images must really mean. If he was real... and he was telling me the truth... then my story had been sustaining a real world. But, either something had gone very wrong... or somehow my story was no longer enough.

When I looked up at him again, he was standing now, looking at me with those strange eyes — eyes that appeared far too hopeful. Then he spoke.

"Time is small."

I let out a breath, rather noisily. "I get that. And I think I've figured out what it is you want from me. But it's not that simple."

"Simple, yes. It is simple. You write. You help. Save them all."

"No, it's not simple. Really." I rubbed a hand over my nose and up toward my forehead. How could I explain this in a way that it would translate? This was ridiculous anyway, since I had no idea how to translate ideas in any way that would make any sort of sense to someone that was most likely an alien.

"I wish I could think of a way to explain to you how this all works." When he said nothing, just waited there looking expectant, I went on. "I can write all the stories I want, but I cannot make them take any of them."

"Take them?" He said the words, and even though they translated somehow, I could both hear and see that he was not getting it, so I tried again.

"How it works is like this. I write a story. It might be wonderful, but I have no way to get the public—other humans—to read it. When I say I can't make them take it, I mean the people who send my story out into the world so that others can read it. They take the story and they make it into a book. People buy that book and read it."

He was nodding now, but I kept going.

"Without a publisher who actually wants to send my story out there, I don't know what to do to actually help."

He started to speak, but I interrupted. "Wait. There have been three other books written about Macus. Have they not helped keep the magic going?"

He didn't nod or shake his head, but he was looking sad before I finished asking the question.

"Those stories you did not write. They are not the same. There is not enough magic with them. Those others do not listen as you do. They write story that is not inspiration."

I didn't even have to ask what he meant. I'd felt the same way myself with each new story that had been published in the series. The same basic elements I had introduced were there, but the world felt flat and dull. The people were the same. But clearly they were simply a tool to get from one page to the next for the ghost-writers who had taken over the writing for those three books. The world obviously didn't feel as real to the new authors as it had to me.

Or... the other authors had simply been writing for a paycheck, not for the love of the story, and the world I had created on paper, and the people in it, that had driven me. If I had to be honest with myself, that felt like the more likely option.

But what could I possibly do about it?

I already knew the answer, of course. There wasn't one thing I could do about it. I had already tried—and failed—more times than I really wanted to think about.

Still... somehow, the memory came to me, strong and fresh, like it had happened yesterday.

I had been at work when I got the first chance to open the official-looking envelope that had come in the mail earlier that day. It was the end of a very long shift, and I figured it would give me an excuse to stay and have a drink with the rest of the staff. Either I would be celebrating or I'd be drowning my sorrows... again.

Up to this point, I had either gotten a nicely-worded rejection letter or no response at all, and since I had sent my manuscript to more than fifty agents and publishers for their consideration, the drowning of my sorrows was coming dangerously close to becoming a weekly occurrence.

But this letter was different. The message inside was not

a polite rejection form. It was not even a show of interest
in seeing more of the work. It was a straight out offer to
buy my book.

chapter three

Even now, looking back at the memory and how excited I had been at the time to have an actual offer, after so many rejections—and how many times I had simply been ignored—it was easy to see how it had all gone so wrong.

When the publisher had offered me $25,000 for my manuscript, with the caveat that I would be selling them the book as a straight sale, to be used in a series to be written by another author already in their employ, I had definitely been confused about what exactly that meant.

But I had also been pretty excited that someone liked the story enough to actually want it and would publish it.

It hadn't occurred to me that they might love the book enough to negotiate, to pay me far more, and royalties to boot. I would never have dreamed what their plan actually was.

How could I have known they intended to promote the book as a new series by a "new" author, with further books being written by ghostwriters they regularly worked with, simply because I did not fit their idea of the type of author who could sell the book to the public?

I had not been born in New York City. I had moved there to go to school and even though I had learned a lot about the under-handed ways of people in general, I would never have imagined just how far the publisher would go to keep so much of the profits they were sure they would net with my book.

How could I have known? I was new to the game then... too new, too trusting, too honest.

It hadn't taken long for me to see what was happening. Unfortunately, when I did, it was too late to do anything about it.

And of course, it hadn't all worked out exactly the way they had hoped. The agent who had signed me as a client after the news had leaked about who this mysterious new writer really was—even though the pen name they had given me was absolutely ridiculous—had gone to some pretty incredible lengths to make certain I had gotten at least a good portion of what should have been mine all along.

Although... he had never been able to convince them to take another of my manuscripts, no matter how many copies the first book sold... and continued to sell.

So, here we were. This stranger was telling me they desperately needed me to write more stories, which was something I had done, but there was no way for me to convince the publishers to actually publish them.

Which left the people of Macus where?

There were no answers. And the stranger in my office was just standing there, looking sad and hopeful, a heart-wrenching combination.

"I'm guessing this is not a normal situation."

He looked shocked for a moment, perhaps at my bold comment... perhaps at my ability to see more than what he had only hinted at until now. I would likely never know. But his answer gave a bit more in the way of hints.

"There is nothing about this that could be normal."

I was nodding already. "You said earlier that I'm not even supposed to know you are here. I'm guessing that the situation is pretty desperate for you to break those kind of rules."

He only nodded in that quick, blurry way.

"And I would guess this has never happened before."

This time it was a shaking of the head, but still quick and blurry movements.

"And, can you only inspire authors?"

Another shake of the head. Good. That's what I wanted to hear.

"Well, then. Perhaps you could find some way to inspire the publisher. Make them realize that it could only be a good thing to use one of my manuscripts."

"That is worth try." This time, it was a nod—he must

have been excited. The movement was so quick, I could barely see his head move.

"All right, then. You do whatever you need to go inspire my publisher—and I'll pull out the manuscript I have that works best. Then I'll send off a message to my agent, tell him to set something up ASAP with the publisher, see if we can get this ball going."

And just like that, he was gone. There was no pop, no fade out, no transition. He was just there one moment and gone the next.

I slowly let out a breath. I was certain all of this would truly begin to sink in soon, and probably throw me for some pretty impressive loops. But in the meantime I would do whatever I could to be ready when the time came.

With that in mind, I turned back to my computer and pulled up the file I had on Macus, determined to read through every single draft I had until I found just the right one.

chapter four

Have you ever had one of those days... one where you felt so completely amazing, that you were convinced that no matter what happened, nothing could go wrong?

Have you ever woken up, having that feeling, and then absolutely everything went wrong. From over-sleeping despite your alarm... to the hot water going out right in the middle of your shower... to the coffee pot actually exploding when you tried to make coffee? Coffee that you've made every day for three years since moving into your house and buying that stupid machine...

Then the weather decides to be freaky, so you arrive, dripping with sweat in the long sleeves and pants outfit you wore because the weatherman predicted the temperatures to fall below thirty. But before you knew it, it was nearly sixty degrees, and you couldn't find a cab and had to walk-run twelve blocks to get to your meeting.

And then, after all of that, the waitress gets everyone's order wrong and when she comes back, she trips and spills an entire bowl of soup—hot soup—on you.

Yeah. This was one of those kind of days. It didn't help that I'd been up half the night, first dealing with some sort of alien messenger asking for my help with something I still didn't have all the details about. And then staying up for several more hours that same night.

First I'd had to find the perfect manuscript to present, and then I'd had to go over it to make certain it was the absolute best it could be. That had taken me all day and half the next night.

I had finally fallen into bed about ten minutes before dawn, planning to get a few hours of sleep before the meeting my agent had excitedly called to inform me about when I was about halfway through editing and polishing my manuscript.

That had not by any means been the first time I'd had to get by with almost no sleep for a couple of days. Over four years of college, there had been more than my share of nights like that, studying and working, plus trying to write in whatever spare time I could manage to scrape together.

In the years since, after selling the one book that brought my unexpected visitor, and then later several books to a different publisher, sleepless nights had become a normal part of my life, especially when a deadline loomed.

And evidently, those long sleepless nights paid off in at least one respect. I'd been told by other authors that worked with my publishers, and by editors who worked for the publishers, that I was a publishing house dream. I was such a perfectionist, that my work needed very little tweaking when I turned it in.

Even the first book I'd sold had garnered the same praise. In fact, they insisted that was one of the reasons for the high price they'd offered me, because they could already see that they would have to do very little to get the book ready to publish.

Not that my agent had ever again allowed one of the shady, under-handed deals that the first publisher had more or less tricked me into.

In point of fact, not only had he done everything he could to change that original contract I had signed, but he had gone above and beyond the call of duty to make certain I got my fair share—if not even more—of the profits from that book.

Fortunately, he was at the restaurant where we had met for lunch to discuss my story idea for the beloved fantasy world that was evidently in such peril.

The visitor—I had no other idea what else to call him—had apparently broken every rule and had shown himself to me, begging for my help. I was still not certain I could be any help to him, or the people of Macus—if they indeed did exist, but he was very convincing, and I was determined to try.

Of course, the way the day was going so far was not helping. The meeting was not going well, even before the waitress had spilled soup all over me.

I wasn't really sure why. I'd been on time, albeit more than a little sweaty and out of breath, likely reminding the publisher's rep just why they had decided not to attribute the book to me in the first place. Instead, they had chosen to use a random pen name to publish the book series under and leaving the author's identity a secret, while using ghost-writers to fill in the series with more books.

Of course, I knew I could never tell them why I was so desperate to have another of my own stories for the series published. Not only would they not believe me, they would likely find some way to have me hustled off, nice and quiet, and locked up somewhere where no members of the media could ever find me.

A part of me had to admit that would not be such a ridiculous thing. I had been working pretty much non-stop for the better part of the last seventy-two hours.

I'd had this unbelievable experience and, instead of dealing with it, I had just taken the strange visitor at his word, and started working the problem.

And it wasn't as if my brain had not come up with all sorts of scenarios where the guy had just been a dream, or else some sort of cosplayer with a really, really great costume.

The worst scenario I could come up with was that I really was out of my mind and I had simply imagined the whole thing.

Of course, I couldn't come up with a single reason why any of those ideas made any more sense than what I so desperately wanted to believe had really happened.

And... yes. There was a tiny part of my brain that wanted it to be true, a small part that wanted me to be the hero who swooped in with my mad writing skills and saved the day, quite literally, for an entire planet.

For now, whether it made sense or not, I was going with that one until someone gave me a really good reason why I shouldn't.

Because... who was I hurting?

No one. However, if it was all true, and I did nothing to help, I would doom an entire planet.

Which might actually happen anyway.

I hated admitting that, even to myself, but I knew it was a very real possibility. They had already rejected every idea I'd brought them.

Just because the story I was bringing them was something they hadn't seen did not guarantee they would treat it any differently than the other three story ideas I had already pitched them over the last five years.

chapter
five

So, when the waitress spilled soup on me, I was tempted to get up and either walk or run out of the restaurant. Just forget the whole thing, go back to my house and shower... again. Then crawl back under the covers and pretend today had never happened.

But I didn't do that.

I sat there, listening to the waitress apologize, and took the towel she brought me. Then I listened to the apology from the manager, who insisted they would pay for the dry-cleaning, and that lunch was on them as well, of course.

Oh. Of course it is. No, actually it isn't. It's on me... all over me, in fact.

I wanted to jump up and scream at them both to be quiet and go away. But I didn't. I just sat there, quietly waiting to see what was going to happen next. I watched as the publisher's rep gave my agent a look that I already knew well enough — too well.

I sat through the remainder of the meal, trying to say the right things, scrambling to make the story sound as amazing to her as it felt to me. Not that it was an easy sell, soaked as I was in what was left over from the tureen of white chicken chili that had taken up residence in my lap so unexpectedly.

It was more than a little difficult, wet and uncomfortable, desperately needing some sleep, while hoping against hope that somehow this would all work out and I would be able to be a hero to a world that might actually exist. Somewhere.

When the overly polite lady from the publisher made it clear the meeting was over, and that there was no chance of them accepting my story, I stood up with everyone, preparing to leave.

I moved to go when they did, but my agent made a point of gesturing for me to stay. I sat back down in my slightly squishy chair and picked up the glass of wine I had yet to finish, as I watched him follow the others out.

While I sat there, slowly drinking the wine, trying to come up with some other answer, or some other option, I looked around the restaurant.

I watched as other people ate their lunch... as they talked, laughed, flirted, texted, and argued. Some of them sat there all alone, like I felt, even though I wasn't actually alone.

I tried to think of what it would be like if our world were the one in danger of extinction. It was harder than I thought to imagine such a scenario.

What would we do? Would we tell everyone? Especially if there was absolutely nothing they could do to help? Would those few of us who knew run around like crazy trying to cram as much living into whatever time we had left as possible?

Would the human race just cease to exist? Would the

entire planet disappear? The thought was simply devastating.

Or would it be something much more dramatic? Would the planet explode... or implode... or die slowly, taking everyone with it as it did so?

How would the people in this room with me react, if it were us?

If we were the world desperately in need of something that some mysterious author somewhere could give us without a moment's hesitation, unless someone in their world would not let them.

How would we handle that?

I had no idea, but I didn't figure it would be especially classy. I had seen enough disaster, and near-disaster movies, to know that when the chips were down, human beings did what was necessary, even when it wasn't pretty or even especially moral.

That was just who we were. At least, according to the movies.

Looking around at the people who sat, completely oblivious to the imminent obliteration of a people so totally dependent on what only someone from our world could provide. They were all wrapped up in their own lives.

And why shouldn't they be? That was what life brought to each and every one of us. Our own worries. Our own woes. Who else was going to solve them, but ourselves?

Not one person in the room, including me, could do a thing right now to help those poor souls. They would have to find some way to survive until another solution could be found.

Hadn't that been what I'd had to do... and what I'd done. Even if not in the best way, I had made my way the best I could, working at whatever jobs I could find until I was finally able to make my way doing what I loved.

Draining the last of the liquid in my glass, I picked up my phone, turned it on, and looked at the time. Figuring I had given Steve the time he would have needed to perhaps work some agent magic I did not possess, I finally made my way to the entrance, where I was met by the manager once more.

I gritted my teeth as he once again repeated everything he had already said about how sorry they were, and how they would certainly take care of my dry-cleaning, and they had made up a to-go bag for me to take home with their compliments... and yet more apologies.

When I saw the bottle tucked inside, along with several food containers that were near to bursting, I held back the acidic response that I had very nearly let loose.

Hey, if they were determined to feed me and pamper me with expensive wine, who was I to argue? After all, I had not spilled the soup on myself.

And when the manager sheepishly started to speak again, but then stopped himself, my curiosity was piqued.

"What is it? Was there something else?"

What else could there possibly be after all of this?

When he pulled one of my books out from behind his back, I nearly laughed out loud, at the irony, at the ridiculousness, at the absolute silliness of the moment, especially since it was the latest book in the series, not even the one I had actually written.

But I had promised the publisher I would do my very best to put a good face on the books. Even if they would not buy any further of my stories, I would not be petty enough to ruin the image every reader had of their much loved author.

He had a pen, and had prepared something he really wanted me to write, which made it all so easy for me. All I had to do was nod, smile, and write a bit.

He was going on about the absolute triumph that was my story. How he positively could not wait for the next book. It had already been too long since the latest books' release. And so on. I kept nodding, and smiling as I signed my ridiculous pen name.

C.W. Starr.

Whoever came up with the ridiculous thing anyway?

Certainly I had not. I had always planned to write under my own name. Though I had to admit, at times I was grateful for the shield to hide behind. It made everything easier.

My house was under my own name. All of my bank accounts. My credit cards. If the publisher had not come up with such an outlandish pen name, I could never have had a moment of peace.

People were lurking often enough when I went out. Or at book signings. Good old C.W. had plenty of people who loved the books. But there were nearly as many who would show up just to give me grief over this or that about the series.

And the worst part was, I could only defend so many of them. Especially when almost all of their complaints were in books I didn't write.

I had to read each book, so I knew what was going on and I could speak intelligently about every part of the story line, but I had only enjoyed one of them so far. And even that one had not quite lived up to my own difficult standards.

Fortunately, this man had no such complaints. He just wanted to heap praise on a favorite author and get her autograph. Once the book was signed and I had again received his heartfelt thanks, I was allowed to escape at last.

I had taken no more than two steps outside the restaurant when an all too familiar voice sounded beside me.

"I do hope your meeting went well." I gasped and turned, suddenly terrified that perhaps I really was losing my mind. I was certain he would not show his obviously alien self to everyone on the street.

Or would he? I mean, he had said he was desperate—truly desperate.

I was more than a little surprised when I turned to look at him. The person standing beside me was a very average-looking man. There was absolutely nothing special—or odd—about him.

Had I imagined it, then? Or had it simply been some sort of clever costume that had fooled me because it was the middle of the night, and I had been more than a little exhausted?

"Yes, it is me. No, you are not seeing things. I cannot exactly appear to these people wearing my true appearance. The reactions from the humans, such as panic and running and screaming, would most certainly make my being here that much more difficult."

I nodded and turned back to continue walking, all the while looking around me to gauge other people's reactions. Were they all seeing this half-strange man walking beside me, alien appearance or not.

It was a tremendous relief to realize that they were — though it was a bit annoying to see that some of the women we passed looked with more than just a passing interest.

If they were seeing what I saw the other night...

I squelched that thought before it could even fully form. If anyone were seeing what I had seen the other night, there would be pandemonium on the streets around us.

That would certainly impede our conversation.

I had to choke back a laugh at the thought. Perhaps my

entire crazed day could be chalked up to a severe lack of sleep after all.

"So, you have some idea what I was thinking when I saw you, but you have no idea that my meeting did not go well?"

I looked at him as I spoke. Even going so far as to stop walking, and turning slightly to face him. I wanted to see if his reaction was as alien as it had been two nights before now.

But there was no reaction. He merely stopped moving, turned to face me, and waited. The all too human features oddly looked out of place to me, knowing now what was really under the facade—a perfect mask of nothing.

I had no way of knowing whether this was proof that he was a very good liar... if his kind even understood what a lie was, or that he simply had no response to my little test.

I turned with a little huff of breath and started walking again. I headed in the general direction of my house, since I had no other destination in mind and I was still by and large covered in soup remnants.

"To answer your question, no. My meeting did not go well. Not at all. They are still very much un-interested in my stories, though they did well enough with the first..."

I trailed off a bit, still struggling to figure out why they purchased the first, but continued to reject any other stories.

I kept walking as I continued to think about it. The strange visitor kept pace with me, never saying a word as I went over it all in my head. No matter how I looked at it, it made no sense.

Maybe in the beginning, when they had planned to keep the author shrouded in mystery. Obviously, they never planned to reveal who the author actually was, mostly because they were convinced I was absolutely the wrong person to be the face of their new series.

Perhaps it made sense for them to reject the stories when they had several others from ghostwriters already lined up. Maybe there were a lot of different reasons they had had in the beginning of all of this.

But with the difference being felt so deeply... not just by readers here, but with whatever connection the work held to this other world.

Not that I can tell them — or anyone — about that.

No, I knew it didn't matter what the reasons were. There was no point in arguing the whys or wherefores. I couldn't make them take the story.

And I couldn't publish anything that was in any way related to the series on my own. The contract wouldn't allow that. I would simply have to find some other way to help the people of my beloved story world. That was the extent of it.

But how to do it? I started to ask the visitor who was still quietly keeping pace with me, but I was reasonably certain he would simply parrot what he had said when last I'd seen him.

Twelve blocks later, I was no closer to an answer than I was when I left the restaurant. I was, however, surprised to hear my agent's voice.

"Aura, dear. I have news."

I turned to smile at the man who had likely only left me behind at the restaurant so that he could make one final plea for my story, absent the mess that I had shown up dragging behind me like a dark cloud.

"Steve, I am so glad to see you're not holding that disaster against me." I stepped forward, but then stopped myself when I remembered the state my clothes were in.

"Oh, how could I possibly hold that against you? It isn't as if you asked that waitress to spill the soup on you."

I laughed for the first time in days... since the strange

visitor had shown up with his quite possibly unreal news. Suddenly remembering him, I was startled to find when I looked around that he was nowhere to be found. I turned back toward Steve.

"True. At least not in such weather." For the first time since I had begun walking, I noticed that the predicted chill had arrived. Fortunately, between the warmth of the restaurant and the waitress's liberal application of towels, my clothes were more stained at the moment than wet from the liquid.

"Yes. It is positively dreadful. You should get inside and change." That was all. No comments on any conversation that had taken place out of my hearing. Nothing about rescheduling. I knew what that meant.

"You couldn't talk them into it." I knew it to be true before he answered me.

"She wouldn't even agree to look over the new manuscript."

I was tempted to stomp my foot. When Steve gave up on something, I knew it truly was a lost cause. There would be no changing their minds.

"And they gave you no indication of why." He said nothing, so I went on. "I mean. It's not as if I'm saying I have such great talent, but it was good enough they took the first book.”

I could hear the frustration rising in my voice, but refused to quit. “After all, they paid a great deal more for the deal than the other authors in the same series were offered. And it isn't as if the follow-up books are getting the same sort of acclaim that mine received.”

Still, Steve said nothing. Something about his manner told me he had more information — details that he was not sharing with me.

“What is it, Steve?”

“It's nothing you need to worry about.”

But I was not giving up that easy. “No. Steve, you know something. I can see you do.”

“It will only upset you.”

“It won't.” I insisted, worried now about what he might know that he felt was not worth sharing... or worse, what it could be that he thought might upset me.

“It's just that in the original contract it says if they buy another of your books for this series, the price and terms for the first book can be renegotiated.”

“You mean this is just about money — for them!” Suddenly, I was angry. If everything the visitor showed me was true, there was a planet full of people who could be dying. And all the stupid idiots who represented the publishing house could think about was money. The heartless jerks.

"I thought you might feel that way. I tried everything I could think of. Told them you've no need of more money for the first book. Told them you're doing just fine with your new books." He looked a bit anxious before continuing.

"But I'm afraid I might have done too good a job with the original re-negotiation we did with them. They're not convinced it isn't all smoke and mirrors."

He was looking down at the ground now, clearly embarrassed that he'd fought so hard for me during the previous negotiations that it was now destroying my chance to sell them a sequel.

"It's all right, Steve. There's no way we could have known this would happen. At the time, it was the best thing you could have done."

"I know how important this is to you, Aura. I can keep trying." He said the words, but there was something in his voice that told me he already knew it would be a waste of time.

I shook my head. "No. Don't worry about that. I think

they've made themselves clear enough. And if we persist, they may just decide they don't need me for any more appearances—and I wouldn't want to disappoint the readers."

He took my hand, then patted it with his other. It might have seemed condescending to some, but to me it had always felt fatherly... and comforting. "That's the spirit, my girl. You have such a good head on your shoulders."

I nodded again. After another pat, he moved his hand. But something must have occurred to him because he put it back almost immediately.

"Oh, I nearly forgot. Now, I know you may not want to think about this quite yet, but Hill House wants to sit down with us, talk about that new series I pitched them last month."

He patted my hand again. "From the sounds of it, you'll be getting your best deal yet from them."

I laughed a little at his words. *The irony*. "Well, at least they like my work."

"Yes, they do. They'll do just about anything at this point to keep you happy, my girl."

I felt like laughing again, but felt Steve might take it wrong, so I cleared my throat instead. "You're right. And

I am grateful to them. They've been a great house to work with."

This time, I reached up and patted his hand. "And it's all thanks to you."

"I appreciate that, but I think we both know it's more thanks to your brilliant work than anything I did."

"How about we agree that it's a perfect partnership, then?" I knew this could easily go on all day. As an agent, Steve seemed to feel it was part of his job to flatter the client.

This might be something that was necessary for most of his authors, but not for me... a fact I had never been able to make him totally aware of. Or else it was just one of those automatic things he couldn't—or wouldn't—turn off because he himself needed it so often.

"Yes. That sounds right. Well, I know you'll want to get inside and change. I'll talk to Hill House and get something set up. Send you an e-mail with the details?"

We both let our hands drop with that, and simultaneously started to move backward, him toward the car he had waiting at the curb, and me toward the steps to my house.

When he was in the car and starting to pull away, I

waved as I moved up one step. Then I nearly stumbled and fell at the voice that sounded just behind me.

"I admit I do not understand. This other publisher will not take your story. Why can this Hill House he spoke of not take your story?"

"Will you please stop doing that!" I spoke sharper than I really meant to, but since my heart was pounding and I had nearly fallen on the concrete steps that led up to my house, I felt more than a little justified.

And while a part of me wanted to laugh at the pure absurdity of it all, at the same time a small part of me wanted to scream. Not only was I taking this alien at his word about what was actually going on in some fantasy world on the other side of the galaxy—as far as I knew, but I was scrambling to find some way to help... when there really was nothing I could do.

And he wanted to ask me questions that I had no idea how to answer. I only knew what the agents and publishing reps told me. I wasn't a lawyer. I couldn't answer questions about such technical things.

With that in mind, I spoke again, my voice sharper than I intended. "I don't know how to explain it, really. You're just going to have to take my word for it when I say they can't."

"Of course. You do not understand either, then. You only know what can and cannot be done."

I breathed a sigh of relief. "Yes. Exactly." And I wanted to smack myself. Why hadn't I thought to answer that way before now?

Because you're a writer, dummy. How often had I remarked that novelists did not do nutshell explanations well?

Every time someone asks me to sum up one of my books.

It made perfect sense now that I thought about it, but it certainly would not have occurred to me otherwise.

What is it about seeing the whole situation only in retrospect?

"All right. So, what do we do now?"

"Is there no other way for you to write the stories of Macus that others can read?"

As we talked, I was moving up the steps. He followed behind me as I unlocked the front door and picked up the mail laying on my foyer floor. Then I headed for the stairs that led to my bedroom on the second floor.

"I can't think of anything. I mean I..." I trailed off as a thought occurred to me.

I moved faster on the stairs, rushing along the hallway

when I reached the second floor. I went past my bedroom and didn't stop moving until I reached the desk in my office.

I sat down and quickly composed an e-mail to Steve. He would probably find it odd that I would be asking about this specific thing, but hopefully he would get back to me soon.

When I'd finished, after going back and re-wording myself several times—I wanted to get this just right—I stopped and turned.

This time I was not surprised to see my alien visitor standing just beside my desk, now looking like he had when I'd first seen him. He said nothing, clearly waiting for me to speak.

So I did.

"Now, this is a long shot, and it may not be possible, but Steve will check out the contract language and get back to me. It may take a few hours or even a day or two, but he will definitely let me know soon."

"And when he does?"

"Well, if he answers the way I hope, there may be a way to put some stories out there, although I cannot guarantee they will get the attention you're hoping for."

"Any attention will be good."

I nodded. "That's what I was hoping you would say." I stood then, let out a little sigh, and stretched muscles I hadn't even realized had been stretched taught.

Evidently, this situation had been knotting me up for days and now that I had a possible solution, I could relax... at least a little.

I headed out of my office, and back down toward my bedroom. In fact, I walked into the room before realizing that the alien was likely still following me. I turned, and sure enough, he was there right behind me.

I cleared my throat before I realized that he would most likely not get the hint that I needed privacy. And just as I expected, he didn't move or make any motion to leave.

"So, um... are you planning to hang around until I hear back from him?"

"Hang around? Why would I hang around?" He looked genuinely perplexed, and on his alien features, the expression was so comical, it was all I could do to quell the urge to laugh.

"I'm sorry. It's an expression. I meant, will you be staying here until I hear back from Steve?"

"It is my plan to stay."

"All right. I get that. But, I kinda need some privacy here. Can you possibly wait downstairs... or in the library? I have lots of great books you can read—if you read."

He didn't answer, so I tried a different approach. "Or, you can help yourself to some food. Do you eat food?"

This time he did answer. "We do not require sustenance such as you do. We acquire energy in a different way."

"All right. But I really do need to shower and change, and I cannot do it with you here in my room."

"I will wait downstairs." And with that, he was gone— again, in an instant.

"I really wish he wouldn't do that." I muttered the words, partly because I had no idea where he'd gone or how close he might still be, and partly because I really didn't want to offend him.

If he was really who—or what—he said he was, and these people really needed me, I was certain I would be dealing with him for some time to come.

I moved into the bathroom, looking all around the room before turning on the water and starting to get undressed, hoping he couldn't see what I was doing. Or would it mean anything to him?

I knew he could sort of read my mind, and could send pictures to my brain, but I had no idea how it all worked. Just thinking about it was making me nervous.

And the last thing I want to do is offend an alien with all sorts of powers... there's no telling what he could do to me if he wanted.

As quickly as I thought it, I shook it off. I stepped under the hot water, focusing instead on the idea I had e-mailed Steve about.

chapter six

When I finally came downstairs, after showering leisurely and dressing in comfortable loungewear, I looked around the foyer and the living area before I spotted the alien visitor in front of the large windows that looked out onto the small yard behind my house.

I noticed right away that he looked human again. Likely a necessity in case one of my neighbors looked out their own window and saw him standing there.

He remained so still, yet somehow he did not resemble a statue. I stood there for what felt like a long time, before I realized I was beginning to view him with my writers' eyes.

I stayed as still as possible, and I made a point of breathing as slowly and quietly as I could as I watched him.

I had so many questions about him... who he really was, where he came from, how he moved so silently, how he managed to pop in and out instantaneously, with no sound or noticeable displacement of air.

And I continued to wonder if he could read my mind. Perhaps he was more of an eternal creature—like an angel—and he had been around for so long, he could visualize what I was thinking by my expression and through past experiences.

Though how much interaction would he have had with humans, if this is something that has never been done before.

And that brought up a whole new round of questions. How was he doing this, communicating with me this way, if it had never been done, and if it were so against the rules? Did he have some sort of special permission or was he really breaking their rules?

And if he was breaking rules, would someone come to

take him away at some point? Would they take me as well because I had seen him as he truly looked? Did I know too much?

And just what is he doing now, standing like a statue for so long, not speaking, not moving. Doing absolutely nothing. Just standing! Is he waiting for something? Is he watching our world —our people? Or is he communicating with others like him. There must be others.

That, at least made some sense. And if he were communicating with others right now, could they be the ones who would have made the rules that he might be breaking?

I wanted to ask him, but I was almost terrified to hear the answers. Somehow, it felt better not knowing, than being faced with some terrible answer.

"You have questions."

I nearly jumped out of my skin at his sudden words, ringing out so clear and strong from across the room, without him ever having moved.

"Yes. I do."

He turned then, still looking human, but I thought I could almost see through the facade. Either he was allowing me to or I was imagining it.

It's as good a place as any to start, I suppose. "I can already guess why you look that way now, just like earlier, but..."

"If I can appear human, why do I not always do so?" He spoke calmly, but his words were so painfully close to what I was thinking, I couldn't help feeling that he was reading my thoughts again.

"Basically, yes. It seems like it would be easier."

"Would you have believed me so easily? If I had appeared to you as any other man?"

I started to answer, but stopped myself. He was right. His appearance, so obviously not human, had definitely played a big part in why I had not questioned him when he'd first shown up. "Okay. You have a point there."

"You have more questions." He said it so pointedly.

A part of me wanted to deny that what he said was true, to not give him the satisfaction of being right. *If he would even feel something like satisfaction.*

I squashed that line of thought. There was no point being petty. He obviously was *not* human. There was no point in expecting him to behave or react like one... or to my reacting to him as if he were.

"Yes, I have more questions. And I'm sure you can see most of them coming, whether you can read my mind or not. Where are you from? Are there more like you? Why me, specifically? Plus, how do you do what you do?"

He started to speak, but I held up a hand. Fortunately, he seemed to know what that meant, so I went on.

"What I really want to know is this. Is there really a point to all of this? If you're breaking rules, is there a chance we will do this, and then it won't end up making a difference? Will they take you away if they discover what you're doing? And what about me? Because if they do, this has all been for nothing."

When he looked at me with an obvious expression, I nodded to show him that I was done speaking for the moment.

"Yes, I am breaking rules. No, there is no one to take you away. No, this has never been done. If you write the story, people read the story. That cannot be taken away."

My shoulders drooped a little as I let out the breath I hadn't even realized I was holding in. And knowing that, I could see that those were the only things I needed to know.

The rest of my questions really weren't all that important. It was just the writer in me, seeking out knowledge, determined to find all the answers.

"You need more answers?"

Clearly he was either reading my mind again or he could see what I had just figured out all on my own. I waved a hand as I sank into the chair that sat just inside the room, behind where I'd been standing all this time.

"Your call. Honestly, I'm not sure I could truly understand it all anyway. You are some sort of alien, I presume. That's probably all that really matters."

"As you wish."

His choice of words brought a smile to my face. I couldn't help thinking about one of my own favorite stories, one where the main character used those words in a significant way.

I jumped again when the cell phone I'd slipped into my pocket loudly rang. My otherworldly visitor made not one move as I pulled the phone from my pocket and clicked the button to answer.

"Hello."

On the other end, Steve's voice came through as almost smug. "Aura, you continue to amaze me, as usual." And he laughed.

I sat there, stunned, confused, trying to decide exactly what had happened for Steve to give me such credit. Had they changed their minds after all?

"This is absolutely the best idea you've had in a long time, dear girl. They will wish they had signed you on for more books when this hits. And I know it will. Your talent is simply staggering. How can it not be huge?"

I thought I knew what he was referring to now, but even so I was almost afraid to ask. What if I was wrong?

"Aura, are you there?"

I realized then that I hadn't said a word since hello. "Yes, I'm here, Steve. So, you think my idea will work?"

"Yes. It will work, and it will be huge! And those snobs will wish they had snatched you up for these stories when they'd had the chance."

The smile returned, spreading across my face then, like a wide, warm hug. I had found the answer. This was going to work.

We're going to save them.

"Well kid, that's really all I wanted to tell you. I'm e-mailing over the particulars. The contract doesn't really deal with this specifically, but there are some bits you should know before you get started. Just look it over and call me if you have questions." He was down to business now.

Good. He won't keep me on the phone.

"That sounds great, Steve. Thank you for jumping right on this. I appreciate it."

"Hey. Anything for my best author."

And before I could say anything else, he went on. "You go get to work. I can hardly wait."

"I will. Thanks again."

With a final "goodbye" he was gone. I pushed the button to disconnect, and looked up at my visitor, who was much closer to me now, although still wearing his human facade.

"He seems to believe it will work. Of course, he doesn't know exactly why I wanted to do it, but if he says it's a go, then I've got a lot of work to do."

He said nothing, but there was a definite light of hope in his expression. I stood up and headed for the stairs, while he followed close behind me.

This was going to work.

Writing is a solitary pursuit. Never let anyone tell you different. And they'll try. Friends. Family. Roommates. Agents.

Strange alien visitors.

They'll all try to look over your shoulder while you work. Only other authors know what a bad idea it is to try and look over the shoulder of an author who is actually writing.

Never let anyone tell you that you should just ignore them. Because you can't. When you're in your fantasy world, living in your characters' skin, it's impossible to do so with someone in the real world standing over you, even if they're not breathing down your neck or casting a shadow on your computer screen.

You know they're there. And it will affect your work, whether you want it to or not. You just might find yourself typing something like "go away or I'm going to have to kill you" where it really doesn't belong in your story.

The funny part about it is that they hardly ever notice when you do. They just stand there and continue to read, even though you've dropped a none too subtle hint, telling them to go away and let you work.

Amazingly enough, an alien visitor—who has already made the point that he is not accustomed to being seen— does the same thing. And, even more shocking, he doesn't take a hint, either. You actually have to tell him to go away.

Twice.

After hanging up the phone, I'd been so excited to get started, I rushed up the stairs, went into my office, sat down at my desk, and had already started typing in a new document before I realized he had followed me—and was standing right behind me, looking down at the page on my computer.

I lifted my fingers off the keys before I could give into temptation, already certain it would not be a good idea to antagonize someone who had unknown supernatural abilities. He might need me, but there was still likely to be a limit to his patience.

Instead, I turned and looked at him, trying to convey with my eyes and body language what I wasn't quite certain how to put into words when there was already a definite language barrier.

He did not take that hint, either.

I hesitated for a moment before realizing that if he really needed my help... and I actually wanted to get anything done—uncertain or not—I would need to be firm.

"I know you are accustomed to not having the subject of your muse seeing you, and all... so maybe you don't realize how distracting it is for you to be there like that."

He straightened, looked right at me, and disappeared.

I turned back to the computer, my fingers hovering over the keys... and nothing came. I sat for what felt like an eternity, just staring at the screen, before I let out a grunt and flexed my fingers in midair.

"That's not helpful." I spoke aloud, fairly certain he was still there somewhere in the room, even though I couldn't see him.

He did not reappear.

"Seriously. I can tell you're still there. Do you want this to work or not?"

He appeared then, right next to me, so quickly, so suddenly, that I jumped backward with a shout, nearly toppling my chair over in the process.

"Don't do that!" I said the words through gritted teeth, rapidly losing patience with the entire situation.

He said nothing. He just stood there, his alien expression impassive, unreadable.

Then, he closed his strange eyes in the way he had once before, and my mind filled with images, some familiar, some not.

I gripped the arms of my chair tightly as wave after wave of images crashed over me. "Don't do that, either." My voice broke as some of the images from the other night, scenes of such desolation and despair that I could hardly breathe, appeared. "It's not helping, and it's not fair."

As quickly as they had begun, the images stopped. I let

out a ragged breath. "Thank you." I took several deep breaths and slowly relaxed the fingers that were gripping the chair so hard, I was beginning to lose feeling in the tips.

He made no move to leave again. Clearly, he felt he needed to be here to inspire the story, so that the magic thing would work. But, I would need something to distract me or I would not get anything done—especially now.

"Do you drink coffee?" Making the decision was easy. Getting out of the house for a bit was always a good way to get the words flowing. And the excellent coffee shop on the corner had been another selling point when I'd bought the house.

I had spent many a day, sitting in that coffee shop, looking out the window at people walking by or watching the patrons inside, making notes in one of the many notebooks I had collected since I'd started writing.

People were an excellent source of ideas. It was one of the unspoken rules about writers. When an author wanted their characters to be realistic, they watched people in the real world.

There was always someone who had some characteristic or a mannerism that reminded you of one character or another. And when you put the two together, the characters in your story simply leapt off the page.

He hadn't answered, so I went on. "I find when I'm having trouble writing, a quick trip to the coffee shop down the block helps clear out the distractions."

Still, he said nothing. But he followed me as I got up from my chair, left the office and headed toward the bedroom to get my purse and notebook.

When he stopped in the foyer, I actually heard his footsteps.

I turned in surprise, "You're welcome to come... or stay. Whatever you prefer. But I need a cup of coffee."

"You have coffee in that room." He pointed one of those long alien fingers toward my kitchen.

A part of me wanted to ask just how he knew what I had in my kitchen, but I did not want to be talked out of going. And there was another part of me that really did not want to know how he knew some of the things he seemed to know.

"It's different," was all I said. I didn't try to explain exactly how it was different, mostly because I didn't really feel the need to justify myself to an alien who had appeared out of nowhere and turned my entire life upside down—and was now trying to take over my life.

I headed for the door. He didn't stop me. He didn't follow me, either. I locked up, just like I always did. Who knew if he would be there when I returned—and I was not about to just leave my home open where anyone could take advantage.

About the time I turned the last key, I realized I was muttering under my breath. I stopped, took a deep breath, squared my shoulders, and turned.

And jumped!

chapter eight

I stumbled back into the door that was now behind me, when I saw the human version of my alien visitor standing not six inches from where I had just been.

"Don't do that!" I stepped back a little, bracing myself against the door, and side-stepped him, turning only slightly toward him before letting loose again. "One of these times, someone is going to see you. And judging by this ridiculous facade..." I swept a hand in front of him.

"Letting people see you do things that regular people cannot do is definitely against their rules. Whoever they are."

He said nothing. Just continued to stand there, looking impassive in that not quite human way that I was becoming far too familiar with.

For some reason, it infuriated me.

I should be celebrating. I should be thrilled. He should be thrilled... if that was even an emotion he could feel.

He should at least feel grateful. That's not too much of a human emotion is it? What am I saying... why should he act human?

Still, it felt like a reasonable expectation to me. I had found a way to help. I could actually do something that would help save the people of Macus.

Or perhaps all human emotions were entirely beyond whatever he was. It shouldn't be a surprise to me. I'd yet to see him display even one human emotion.

Somewhere in the back of my mind, that little voice you hear right before you do something you're not supposed to, reminded me that I had seen a human emotion from him—one of the most intense of the emotions that we felt. Grief.

The very first time we had met, he'd clearly been

grieving for the people of Macus—or at least the world of Macus—when he'd shown me how my beloved world had changed. Or maybe those images were supposed to be how it could change if they did not get an infusion of magic... and fast.

He'd never said. At the time, I had been too overwhelmed to ask.

Which brought to mind another thing that was frustrating me at the moment. Steve's call had interrupted his answering at least some of my questions. Questions that would likely continue to distract me until I had some answers.

I couldn't be annoyed with Steve. He had been right on top of the situation, and I was grateful to him for jumping on it so quickly. However, in my excitement, I had missed out on getting any more answers from my strange alien visitor.

And now he was hovering.

Likely, he figured he would get results out of me quicker if he hung round and put the pressure on. Somehow, I would have to make him aware that doing so would be the worst possible way to actually get me to do any decent writing, of any sort.

Since he still hadn't moved, I took the initiative. I

walked down the steps and turned toward the end of the block. Several steps later, I realized I was muttering under my breath again.

With a grunt of frustration, I stopped myself and turned, nearly knocking down an actual person who just happened to be walking behind me at the moment.

The human version of my strange alien visitor was, of course, nowhere to be seen. It was quickly becoming obvious that was his MO. Never around when I expected him. Always around when I didn't.

To the person I had nearly knocked over, I sputtered out an apology, which he waved away with a reassurance that he was just fine. He stepped around me and continued on his way.

I didn't know his name, but I did recognize him as someone who I sometimes noticed at the coffee shop. He always ordered a black coffee and a muffin, but he never stayed to eat or drink. And it was pretty much the only interaction we'd ever had until now.

Since he had headed off in the direction of the coffee shop, I hurried to catch up.

"Are you headed to the coffee shop, by any chance?"

He looked at me, nodded, but didn't stop walking. I

rushed on, still scrambling a little to catch up with his long, quick strides.

"As part of my apology, can I buy you a coffee. Or a muffin. Or both." I was breathless now, but determined to keep up with him.

He stopped suddenly, turned and frowned at me. "How do you know what I was going to order at the coffee shop?" His voice sounded gruff, but thankfully not angry.

"Mostly because that's what you order whenever I see you there." Before he could say anything else, I rushed on. "I'm there a lot and I tend to watch people. I've seen you there and that's all you ever order. I figured it was a safe bet." I shrugged, hoping he would take me at my word... and not think I was some sort of psycho.

This was New York City, after all.

"Well, I can't say that I've ever seen you there, but I have seen you going by my house sometimes. You always seem to be in a hurry." He sounded a little less suspicious and a little amused.

"Me? In a hurry?" Since the words came out on a gasp of breath and I panted a little after I said it, I could only hope he would realize that I was trying to make a joke and not think anything weird... or at least, nothing more weird than he already might.

Thankfully, he laughed. "I see your point."

He slowed down a little. "I'm not often keeping pace with someone."

I thought he sounded just a little sad as he said it, but I had no idea how to respond. I knew I could try to make another joke, but since most people did not understand my quirky sense of humor, I could just bum him out more, so I said nothing.

It feels safer to just play along.

About four steps later, we reached the coffee shop. My strange alien visitor in human disguise was still nowhere to be seen. My still nameless neighbor reached to open the door for me. I smiled and walked in ahead of him.

His long legs carried him into the store, quickly catching up to me, and we stepped up together to the end of the line.

After a minute, I started to feel the beginning of an uncomfortable silence. "So, have you lived here long?"

"Ten years. You?"

"I've just been here two, so far. I like it. It's a good neighborhood." I answered a little absentmindedly as I looked at the handwritten chalkboard standing at the end of the counter. It always had some clever saying about the coffee blend of the day and any specials they were running.

The only thing it said today was "I see London. I see France. I see French Roast... coffee. Try some." I wrinkled my nose a little bit at the thought of it.

"You don't like the French Roast? Or is it the bad pun?"

I laughed. Maybe he would understand my strange sense of humor after all. "The French Roast. Not a fan."

"Do you have a favorite blend, then?"

I laughed again. "Nothing so cut and dried as that. I'm what you might call a coffee wimp."

He looked at me quizzically, and I went on quickly. "I prefer my coffee sweet, flavored, and mostly blended into something more like a milkshake. Though I do enjoy a good white chocolate mocha when I really want hot coffee."

Now he was laughing. "Yeah. I can see why my basic, plain black coffee would catch your attention then. You probably cringe whenever anyone orders one."

I swatted his arm lightly. "I'm not quite that bad, thank you."

He grinned, but I insisted. "I have no objection to other

people drinking their coffee however they like. I just want the same freedom." After a second I added, "without judgement, preferably."

He laughed again. "That sounds like someone in your past has made judgements about your coffee preferences."

I nodded. "More than one."

I held up fingers as I went through the list of names. "My mom. My dad. Several boyfriends. My grandfather. And my doctor."

He leaned back a little at the last one, his expression quizzical again. "Your doctor?"

"Too much sugar."

He laughed again. "Okay. I suppose I understand that. Still, you look plenty healthy to me. Is he one of those young doctors who thinks everyone should be stick thin and eat nothing but vegetables all day?"

I laughed then. "No, actually. He's my dad's age and he..." I put both hands up in air quotes as I went on. "...worries about me."

We both laughed at that.

When we stepped up to the counter, my still nameless neighbor gestured for me to order first. So I did. Since it was still warmer outside than it ought to have been, I ordered one of the milkshake-like concoctions I had only been half joking about earlier, plus a scone.

He ordered his usual black coffee and muffin, choosing blueberry today. Then he pushed my hand away when I reached into my bag for my wallet.

"But I said I'd pay. And I did bump into you."

He was shaking his head with a mischievous little smile. "There may not be many of us left in this crazy world, but any man who considers himself a gentleman would never allow a pretty lady to pay for a meal they are sharing with us."

I laughed, more at his phrasing than anything specifically he'd said. "Okay. You have a point there."

"I know. Right? It's frightening just how few of us remain."

He said it so seriously, I couldn't help but laugh again.

We both turned at the sound of our orders being called out and walked together side-by-side to the counter. He handed me my coffee drink and the tiny plate with my scone on it before turning back to take his coffee and the small plate where his muffin rested. I actually started to wonder if he would accompany me to a table, but before I could even move toward one, he leaned across the counter and spoke to the barista.

"Could I possibly get a bag for this muffin and a lid for the coffee?"

So, he would be going... like always. I wondered why that thought made me sad all of a sudden.

When the young woman behind the counter handed him his lid and bag, I shook myself a little. It would not do to have a sour face on when he turned. It had been a nice walk and some nice conversation along the way.

And I didn't exactly have any claims on his time.

He turned a moment later with a smile. "Well, this was nice." And he gestured toward the door with his shoulder, "Guess I should be going."

"Yeah. I'm just gonna..." I trailed off, but shrugged behind me toward the few empty tables. "It was nice bumping into you."

He laughed a little. "Yeah. We should do it again sometime." And then he turned and was weaving his way out of the busy coffee shop. After going through the open door, he turned and held it open for the person behind him. Then as he let go of the door, he held his hand up in a half wave, before turning away.

I turned back toward the dining area, looking for an empty table. There weren't many today.

Then I noticed him. Honestly, I probably should have felt surprised to see my alien visitor sitting at one of them, disguised as a human again, with a cup of something sitting on the table in front of him... though it looked as if he had not touched it.

I walked over to the table, stopping when I was standing right beside him, but did not sit down. When he looked up at me, I sighed. "Is this just how it's going to be now? You'll follow me everywhere? Or else turn up wherever I am?"

He said nothing. A habit that was beginning to get on my nerves. When I continued to stand, he finally spoke.

"There is much work to be done."

"I know." I also knew my voice was a bit sharp, but I didn't much care at the moment. I was stressing over several things. And the coffee shop, where I usually went to de-stress, was feeling more confining and stressful by the second.

"You have your coffee." He moved his head toward my cup, much slower than I was becoming accustomed to seeing, but still a bit quicker than other humans would expect. I looked around the coffee shop.

Thankfully no one was watching us.

There were far too many people in the room, with all their attention centered on their phones or laptops, to notice anything going on around them. But I had a bad feeling that if we stayed much longer, he was certain to do something not quite human, and he could attract the wrong sort of attention in here far too easily.

Besides which, since I wasn't alone, I really wasn't enjoying being here anymore. "Okay. Let's go, then."

He stood, again moving too fast, too smooth. Fortunately, enough people nearby were engrossed in whatever they were doing, so no one seemed to notice. Not yet anyway.

Almost immediately, I wondered why I was so concerned about what happened with the strange alien who had appeared so abruptly and turned my life inside out and upside down. Yes, I believed him when he said he needed my help.

But that did not make me his keeper.

He had no problem appearing and disappearing at will. If someone took too much notice of him, I was certain he could get himself gone before any government men showed up to cause him trouble.

And why was I letting it all get to me so much anyway. I was a writer. It was not my job to worry about aliens or save people who were somewhere on the other side of the galaxy... or in some other dimension that no one on earth even knew about.

If I could help them by writing, then I would do that. But I vowed right then and there that I was not going to let all of this make me crazy... not anymore.

I stepped out of the coffee shop feeling much more like myself. I was feeling less stressed now, and oddly, ready to do some serious writing.

When I looked around for my alien tag-along, of course he was nowhere to be seen. I laughed, shrugged my shoulders and headed back down the sidewalk toward my house.

I did not encounter anyone on the walk home. Not my still nameless neighbor, nor the strange visitor that had seemed so determined to get me on track only a few minutes ago.

Perhaps he can take a hint after all.

I smiled to myself. I was beginning to think he was a lot more like us humans than he wanted me to know.

Keeping secrets. Pretending to be so unemotional.

Refusing to rise to even the smallest piece of bait.

Yes, much more human than he is letting on.

I was laughing when I opened the door to my house. I walked in, set my purse on the little table beside the door and turned to lock the door.

I never even managed to turn the latch on the deadbolt.

Strong arms came around me and held tight. A moment later, something was sprayed into my face. I held my breath, but it didn't make a bit of difference. Whatever they'd sprayed was fast acting, without my even breathing it in.

As darkness closed in around me, I tried to fight the arms holding me.

If I could just get outside...

chapter nine

When the darkness began to fade, I was sitting on something soft. The tight hold around my midsection was gone. And I did not feel any of the effects I had thought to expect from someone having knocked me out.

I'd written more than one scene in my books where someone was chloroformed or hit over the head. They always awoke groggy and disoriented... and usually with a massive headache.

I had none of that. I knew immediately where I was. I was in my own living room, on the couch, covered with a throw that had been folded neatly and lying over the back of the same couch only this morning.

If it had indeed been only this morning. There was nothing in the room to tell me if a few hours had passed... or if it had perhaps been days. I looked carefully around the room, having no way of knowing whether or not the person who had done this was still around.

I didn't have long to wonder. Someone was standing beside the couch. His back was to me, but there was something disturbingly familiar about the hands that were resting against his side.

As I looked further around the room, I could see that there were more of them — at least five that I could see.

And likely more where I cannot see them.

That made sense. They wouldn't just be in this one room. They would be all over the house, probably going through my things. Learning everything about what I had been up to over the past few days. And, depending on how long it had been, they likely knew everything that had happened since *he* had first shown up.

So, this is it then.

All of my earlier fears came crashing back, drowning me with worry and a sick feeling that started in the pit of my stomach and spread out everywhere.

I had a moment to wonder why I was still here, in my house, on my couch, unbound... before my imagination took over.

I began to wonder if I was about to become one of those mysterious deaths people read about in one of the sensationalist tabloid style magazines. One that would never be solved, because who would think to look for an alien killer...

Especially one who can appear and disappear at will.

Since no one had paid any attention to me yet, I took my time studying the others standing in the room with me. They all had the same strange fingers, the same too-still posture. I could not see their faces, but I was certain I would find the same overly-large eyes and odd looking mouth if I could have.

Not one of them moved even a little, which reminded me of the stranger who still had yet to identify himself to me.

And likely never will.

They all stood as still as statues in their places around

the room, and it was impossible to determine whether they were waiting for something or just making certain I did not escape. They might not be looking right at me, but somehow I knew they didn't need to.

I could slide as quietly as possible off the couch and make a rush for the door, but with so many of them here... and that disappearing thing they did...

Well... I wasn't exactly fast anyway.

I knew I had about as much chance of reaching the door as I did of winning the lottery without ever having bought a ticket. So, I waited.

Whatever was coming was most likely inescapable. And I most certainly would not want to give them any reason to be any more cruel about it than was absolutely necessary.

Yet, as I sat there, I had plenty of time to wonder over things. Time passed slowly, stretching out and giving me plenty of time to wish I had never gotten involved in this whole business. Though how I could have managed that was a mystery to me. I mean, who could have stopped it? For certain, I hadn't asked a strange alien to visit me and start this whole mess I was in.

Suddenly, the thought made me angry. I hadn't asked for this. How dare they act as if I did. I was just here... in my life… minding my own business. I was not bothering them one bit.

It's not as if I could have known what was going on. Because I had no clue until *he* showed up and told me everything.

And did I ask for a single shred of proof? No, I did not.

I had gone right along with him, believing every word he had said, taking it as fact that he knew what he was talking about and that I was important to him and this world I had always imagined that I had created in my story.

Not exactly feeling important now.

The thought occurred to me though that perhaps this also had something to do with my not having been as successful as they wanted.

It's not as if I didn't go on writing about the stupid world though.

I *had* written about it. Even when I had written other stories in several different series. Stories that had been published. And stories that would not leave me alone until I had written them down.

I can't very well make them take the stories and publish them.

And he knew that. I had explained that I couldn't. He

knew I had tried. He knew I had done everything I could think of to get it going.

And... when the publisher had not gone for it, I had figured out another way to do it. I just hadn't had the time to get started yet. Could I help it that he'd driven me mad with his hovering?

I just went for a stupid cup of coffee. I was coming right back.

I was so certain I had the explanation now. They must be here because I had not done what was needed, and something was going terribly wrong with the world.

He had said the situation was becoming desperate.

But then I'd gotten the idea of how to get the stories published. I'd done what was necessary to get started. And he had been right there, looking over my shoulder.

If he had been inspiring the stories within me for years, he should have known that I couldn't write like that.

How could he have known though, when that was all he ever did? How could he know the difference between me knowing he was there — and not knowing he was there?

There was that same little voice... reminding me of what I really already knew to be true.

For all my thinking that he was more like humans than I

expected, the truth of it was that he wasn't human. How could I expect him to know when it was all right for him to hover nearby, invisible and unknown, and when it wasn't—when he was visible and practically breathing down my neck.

I can't.

And that was the extent of it. There was nothing I could do about any of this that I had not already done. And that was when the anger really started flowing, rushing through veins that had gone cold as ice water, burning... seething... practically making me see red.

I had believed an impossible thing—with no proof.

I had done everything that was asked of me. I had found a way to make an impossible request actually possible. And now I was being held responsible for something which I had no responsibility in.

So none of this is my fault.

In fact, I was the only one who had actually done something to fix the whole mess. He had said he would go and inspire the publisher to want my story.

He hadn't.

More anger. This time thinking back to the disastrous meeting in that stupid, fancy restaurant. I had rushed and ran and shown up to my meeting dripping sweat and exhausted. I'd had soup spilled on me. I'd had everything that possibly could to go wrong that morning.

And he had not managed to inspire them to do anything differently than they had ever done where I was concerned. They had treated me just as they had from the very beginning. Which was pretty much horribly.

Then why exactly is it me who is being punished!

And with that thought, I very nearly pushed myself off the couch in anger.

But I never got the chance.

Just when I had decided to stand up, full of anger, out of frustration and annoyance... another one of them popped into the room, right in front of me. And he did not look happy at all.

Not that I know what happy looks like on them.

I just knew this was not it.

He stood there, glaring—there was no other word for it —at me. He was also doing that same looking right through me thing my alien visitor had done when he'd first appeared to me.

If any of them can read minds, this one obviously can.

And shockingly, when I thought about it, his expression changed, ever so slightly—so quickly I barely caught sight of it.

I knew it.

What happened next would have knocked me back on my rear, had I actually stood up a few moments earlier.

"You know things about us that you should not know. How is this?"

It was just like the images that the other alien visitor, the nice one, had put into my mind. Only it was clearly speech from the alien standing in front of me, if my guess was correct. And it was translated, just like the other's speech was. Only, now I was only hearing the translation... in my head.

"You can read my mind. Shouldn't you know the answer to that?"

His very alien scowl deepened, then darkened. But he said nothing, and pushed no thoughts into my head. He only stood there, scowling at me.

Clearly, he couldn't read *all* of my thoughts. Because if he could, he would know that I was not so easily intimidated.

"We are not here to intimidate you."

Immediately, I shot back a reply. *"Well, then you're doing a really crappy job of whatever it is you are here for."*

Later I would focus on how this all worked, realize that he could probably only read certain thoughts... or really loud thoughts... or something. But right now, all I could think was that I'd had enough of this. I had work to do and no patience for even more aliens to be barging into my life.

"This is why we are here. You have met one of us."

"Uh huh." And in that moment, distracted by his unexpected proclamation in my mind, I spoke aloud... more out of habit than anything else. Why didn't he seem to know that one of theirs had come to visit me?

Of course. I realized then. *Well... hmm.* Maybe this wasn't just about my not working fast enough. Maybe it was more about what *he'd* done. He had said he was breaking the rules.

And here were the consequences. Just like I had known there would be. Just like I had said there would be.

I had seen enough movies to know that whatever came next would not be good. And that there would be nothing I could do about it.

Or do to stop it.

I sat back against the couch, crossed my arms and waited for whatever was about to happen. This new alien might have me at a disadvantage, but I was not going to sit here shaking and frightened. Although that same tiny voice reminded me of why I was in this position to begin with.

Those poor people.

No one would be able to help them now. He'd already said my writing was what made the magic work the way the world needed. Without me to write the stories, what would happen to them?

The memories of what I had been shown flitted through my mind. First, the beautiful world I had imagined, that I had written about, that I had been certain I had made up.

Then the images of devastation and death that made me feel as if I might be sick to my stomach. I gritted my teeth against the tears that threatened to betray my determination to stay cold and aloof.

Suddenly, all of the aliens, except for the one directly in front of me, vanished.

I looked around, wondering where they had gone... wondering if this was some part of their punishment process. Would they hide from me so I couldn't see them coming?

Or were they actually gone?

And if they were gone, where had they gone? And why? Why now? What had happened? What had I missed?

It was then that I saw the one I considered *my* alien visitor. He stood in the doorway, looking as alien as I had ever seen him—even more than he had appeared to me before. He looked even more alien than the one who still stood in front of me. The one who, when I looked up at him, saw that he was now looking where I had just been.

His expression changed lightning quick several times in the space of just a few seconds. And he was looking at the other alien so intently, I was certain they must be communicating, in that strange telepathic way they had.

And then they stopped. And the original alien visitor—my alien visitor—was standing right beside the new one. Both of them stood directly in front of me now, side by side, the first having moved so quickly, I hadn't even seen it. One second he'd been in the doorway. The next he was standing in front of me. He had just... poofed. Appeared.

They were both looking at me now. I looked right back at them. The determination was back. If something was going to happen, I was going to meet it head on. No whimpering or begging for me.

They would be the ones ultimately who would regret it

if anything happened to me. Because the world they cared about would run out of magic... and soon, from the sound of things.

"You have much to do." The words sounded in my head, and I was pretty sure it was the new alien speaking... thinking... them.

I answered the same way—in my thoughts. *"Yes, I do."*

He made a gesture that was about as close to a nod as they got. And then he was gone.

And then I was alone, or it looked that way to me, with the original alien who had been complicating my life for the last couple of days... days that felt more like years when I stopped and thought about all that had happened.

Has it really only been two days since this crazy alien popped into my life?

It felt impossible that so much had happened in such a tiny amount of time. How could that be right?

"Time is not something your people understand."

Now it was his words in my head. And right away I noticed differences in the sound, in the tone, and in the way the words sounded.

"I knew you could read minds." I knew that I sounded smug,

but I didn't really care. After what I had just been through, I was entitled to be a little smug... and a lot annoyed... and in need of a drink.

Getting to my feet, I moved forward slowly, on legs that were a lot more wobbly than I wanted to admit, and walked to the kitchen. There, on the counter, stood the bag from the restaurant I had put down only hours before —although I still wasn't sure how much time had passed since I arrived back home from the coffee shop.

I pulled the bottle out of the bag and judged it to be too warm to drink now. Looking at the label, I could see this was something I would want for a better occasion anyway. A time when I could actually enjoy drinking it.

So, I turned and opened my fridge. Fortunately, there was a bottle I had opened a few days earlier. I took it from the shelf that ran along the width of the door and went in search of a wine glass.

My alien visitor watched from the doorway. I might have said there was something akin to amusement on his features, but I wasn't sure you could call it that.

"You understand much."

The thought popped into my head suddenly. But it was passive, and I was becoming more accustomed to it than I ever would have thought possible.

I didn't bobble the wine glass or the bottle. Just continued on with the business of opening the bottle and pouring wine into the glass, before turning back to him.

"And you underestimate me."

He did that quick little head bob I thought must be a nod. *"You are strong."*

I wasn't sure what to make of that, but something about it made me want to laugh... perhaps it was the irony. He was telling me I was strong, and I was pouring a drink for my nerves that felt as if they just might shake free of my body at any moment.

"I don't feel strong."

"You are." His words sounded in my head, but after a second, he spoke aloud... once again in that strange double layer of speech.

"There is much that you learn in a short amount of what you call time. You do not run. You do not deny. You do what is asked. You stay when frightened. You defy."

"I don't feel strong." I repeated the words just before taking a long drink from the glass in my hand.

"You underestimate you."

Again, the words just sounded in my head.

That brought a smile to my face. I could see I was not going to win this fight. I was stuck with it. Just like I was stuck with what he was asking of me.

I was stuck with him. I was stuck with this duty. I was stuck with this mission. And I was stuck with what he thought of me.

"Okay. Maybe I'm stronger than I think I am."

"This is why you are powerful. This is why you must write the words."

That, I could believe.

"Okay, then. Let's do this." I pushed away from the counter, still carrying both the wine glass and the bottle, and headed for the stairs.

He silently followed.

chapter ten

Did you know that writing is not actually considered a job by a lot of people? No. Really, it's the truth. Most of my relatives do not consider what I do to be a job.

They say things like, "It's good you're having fun with your little hobby, but when are you going to get a real job?" with shocking regularity.

Family holiday get-togethers are a nightmare for me. Which is why I don't always go. I sit at home and write —

which, when weighed against dealing with all of the family drama and the barrage of questions and opinions about my work, is really what I would rather be doing anyway.

Fortunately, writing can also be an escape. It may be wishful thinking on my part, but I like to believe that most people would not be able to deal with the sorts of things that we writers do—and still do their job.

We have unrealistic deadlines, sleepless nights, research nightmares, writer's block, unsupportive families, plus actual voices and visions in our heads... that we then rush to put down on paper, turning those voices into as real people as we can manage in a ridiculously short amount of time.

Some of us also deal with strange alien visitors, uncooperative publishers, and the threat of possible harm from still more strange alien visitors who turn up unexpected and uninvited in our homes to frighten us.

Oh, sorry. I forgot. That's just me.

My point is, as a writer, I take those experiences and funnel them into my writing, using them as a lightning rod to actually power the words I fill pages with.

And I like to believe that a banker or a lawyer would not have the same ease of returning to their job... as if nothing at all had happened... as if they had not just been frightened half to death and feared their own death so seriously for several minutes, their heart had actually felt in danger of actually stopping all on its own, with no help from aliens or humans alike.

But that's just my own hopeless wishful thinking.

The point is, when faced with what I was convinced was almost certain death, I stood... or sat, really... and did not back down. I didn't whimper or beg.

I was quite proud of myself actually.

Of course, the very moment they were gone, if indeed they were actually gone and not just invisible somewhere watching me — but I resolved not to think of that. At any rate, the moment they were gone, I retreated to my good friend, my loyal and steadfast companion. Wine.

Wine never lets me down. It also has a way of giving me extra courage to deal with things. And, fortunately, I have such a hearty constitution, it takes a lot to really affect me.

Unfortunately, after my experience with the rest of my alien visitors... whose names I really needed to learn... I finished off a bottle that had been mostly full when I pulled it out of the fridge.

I took it upstairs. And I did write.

What I found the next morning, when I woke up, all alone, still completely dressed and laying crossways on my bed, with my pillows tangled up with me where I must have pulled them, or else just crawled in between them when the wine had done me in, was more than a bit of a mess.

The writer in me had me going to see what I had written, if anything, before doing anything else—even showering.

My laptop was in rest mode, thankfully, with the lid still open and standing proudly upright. Just as I began tapping out my login, I saw an error message. I dove for the cord, plugging it in as quickly as my fumbling fingers could manage.

Then I logged in.

The words in front of me might actually be words, and they truly might—if someone were being extremely generous, be considered to be sentences, but they made no sense whatsoever.

Looking at the top of the document, I was relieved at least, to see that I had started on a fresh document—and not written over some other story I had been working on.

I considered, for more than a moment, simply hitting the *delete all* option. However, curiosity got the better of me and I decided to save the insanity. There might be something within the mass of semi-conscious rambling that was worth salvaging.

So, I dutifully saved the document and then went in search of a shower.

chapter eleven

Nearly an hour later, I was showered, dressed, and somehow miraculously minus a hangover. I made my way downstairs first. Coffee was certainly the first order of the day.

And that is—ironically—where I encountered my strange alien visitor.

He was in the kitchen, looking oddly human again and leaning against the counter as if he lived there. When I opened my mouth to ask why he was here, in the kitchen, looking the way that he did, he put a finger to his lips in such a familiar way, that I stopped, stepped back and waited.

I didn't have to wait long.

Not thirty seconds after I'd entered the kitchen, grateful that I did not have a hangover to deal with, I started to get a headache, as I always did when I had to deal with my youngest sister.

She breezed into the kitchen beside me, her voice its' usual high-pitched, chirpy annoyance that every person in the world who is not a morning person finds unbearable the first thing after waking.

"Hey there, sleepyhead." She positively sang out the words as she moved past me and toward the counter, where she picked up the cup that I had not previously noticed sitting there.

"Are you aware that it's already ten? Just how late were you up last night?"

I answered absently as I moved to where the coffee maker stood. "I honestly have no idea."

Grinding my teeth a little when I discovered the pot was empty, I went about the business of making coffee. *She's probably drinking tea. Who in their right mind drinks tea in the morning?*

My suspicions were confirmed a moment later, when I spotted my tea kettle sitting on the stovetop.

It could only be there if she had put it there. And, of course she knew exactly where to find it. It was all she ever drank.

I half-listened to her annoyingly chirpy admonitions about late nights and even later mornings while I shoved a fresh filter into place, dumped coffee grounds inside, and then waited impatiently for enough water to pour out of the bottle on the counter into the pitcher I used to transfer water to the reservoir on the coffee maker.

Only when said coffee maker was making sounds that told me my life-blood was brewing, did I turn to face her.

"How are things with you, Leda?" I asked the question to be polite, but I was already fairly certain I did not want to know the answer.

Typically, when Leda showed up unannounced somewhere, she needed money. And, when that somewhere was here, it meant she had already asked everyone else in the family worth asking — and had either been told no... or she needed more than everyone else had already agreed to part with.

"Can't a girl just drop in to see her dear sister?" She looked down at the mug she held, not just refusing to meet my eyes, but not even looking up anywhere near my face.

This was not a good sign.

"How much?" I was done beating around the bush. I knew what she wanted. I had work to do. I was in no mood to deal with her little games.

She sighed... loudly, but didn't look up. "Oh, Aura. Come on. Why do you always just assume I want money?"

"Because you do. And this is how I know. You come here, let yourself in, help yourself to my kitchen, and then lecture me — in my own home — about my work hours."

"Work. Ha." She exclaimed. Her volume had me clutching at the sudden pain in my head. Hangover or not, she was entirely too loud for first thing in the morning.

She made no attempt to be quieter or less cheerful. In fact, her next words were filled with entirely too much glee, as if she had caught me with a hand in the cookie jar.

"You. Are. Hungover."

She said each word with such finality, they were each

like a little sentence, said in an ever-increasing volume.

"You haven't been working on anything but finishing off a bottle of wine." She looked up then, suddenly empowered by the lie she wrongly assumed she'd caught me in.

I exhaled loudly before answering, my annoyance leaking into my tone and the words I chose as well. "I didn't say anything about whether or not I had been working. I said you give me grief about my work hours."

The coffee maker chose that moment to beep, announcing that it had finished brewing. I pounced on it like a drowning woman coming up for air.

"And, since this is my home, and I am well over the legal drinking age, I don't see that you have anything to say about how I chose to spend my nights." I muttered the last bit mostly under my breath, but it was too late.

She knew she'd hit a nerve. "Touchy."

Waiting, I took several long sips of coffee, hoping the fog that filled my brain would clear just a little. I might not be hungover, as she had accused me, but I had never been a morning person and I had to work to be clever under the best of circumstances.

When I said nothing, she took the opportunity. "For

your information, I was coming to let you know that Mom is planning to sell the house."

I waited, but she said nothing else until I said, "Yes... and?"

"And, I was hoping you would help me talk her out of it."

She set down the mug and leaned against the counter, crossing her arms over her chest with a look that was likely to mean I was especially slow not to have known immediately where she had been going with her first comment.

I took another sip of coffee, a larger one this time due to the cooling temperature, but nothing about her comments made sense to me. What did it matter to her whether or not Mom sold the house?

When I said as much, her only response was a huff and a glare.

"All right. You can stand there and glare at me or you can explain. Which do you think will actually get results?"

She uncrossed her arms and picked up her discarded mug, taking a long drink before answering. "Well, it's only the house we all grew up in."

I could tell from her tone—and her behavior—that something was bothering her, but somehow, I didn't think it was what she was saying.

Evidently, she figured it out at the same time, and apparently, had no intention of explaining further. She took one last drink from her mug, set it back down, and headed for the front door.

I followed, curious to see if she was actually going to leave or just make it look like she was.

For some reason, she must have decided she was not going to get whatever it was she wanted from me. Because after one last withering stare over her shoulder, she picked up the large shoulder bag that she'd dropped on my hall table, and opened the front door.

Then she stormed through it, pulling it shut behind her. Hard. Loud.

"I want my key back." I muttered at the closed door, knowing it would do no good. Even if she'd heard me, it wouldn't change a thing.

She might give me back the key I had given her, but I had a feeling she'd made other copies.

I stood there for several minutes, watching the door, waiting to see if she would come back and blast me with another tirade.

She didn't.

I stood there for another minute, indulging in a fit of the childishness. She always seemed to bring one out in me. I stuck out my tongue. I stomped my foot several times, setting down my coffee mug when I came dangerously close to spilling its contents on the floor in front of me.

I made faces at the door and then wiggled my fingers from my ears while I stuck out my tongue at the door again. It didn't open, and there was no indication it would, even after several minutes of my just standing there watching it.

So, I determined to shake off the craziness and get to work. With a shrug, I went to pour myself another cup of coffee before heading back upstairs. But not before locking the front door.

Not that it would do any good.

It was only when I walked into the office, and saw my alien visitor sitting in the same chair where he had first appeared to me, that I realized my sister had never asked me about him.

Even though he had looked human, she must have seen him.

Oh dear, had she seen him? She must have.

But I already knew the answer. Had she wondered about him? Why he was here? Where he'd gone when we started talking? If she had, then why hadn't she asked me anything about him? And when had he come upstairs anyway?

Without my having said a word to him, he answered my questions. Out loud.

"She did not see me. I took on the human guise when she came in, but she did not pay me any attention. You came down. I came up."

And that was it. Short and simple.

So, she hadn't seen him.

Or had she—and she simply hadn't cared enough to ask about him?

It should have made me feel better, knowing she hadn't paid any attention to him. But strangely, it did not. Nothing about the entire visit gave me anything to feel good about.

I stood there and sipped my coffee, wondering about it all. Every part of it. None of it made sense.

My sister letting herself into my house. That made sense. But leaving so quickly, and without asking for any money. That never happened before. So why now?

If she truly had not seen the alien, looking human but still there in my house. If she really had not seen him, then it made sense she wouldn't have said anything to me. But, my sister paying no attention to someone as good looking as his human facade was... well, that was pretty much impossible!

Also, what she had said about Mom selling the house we had grown up in. That made no sense, either. No matter how I looked at it. We had tried to talk her into selling it so many times over the years. The answer had always been the same. It was her house. It was where she had lived for forty years. Where her babies had grown up. She could never leave her home.

So, why now, so suddenly and completely out of nowhere, would she suddenly decide to sell the house? And why was Leda so upset about it? She had left that house the very instant she could and she had never moved back, no matter how desperate she'd been for money.

Why would she care if Mom sold the house?

I would likely never know. Clearly, she wasn't about to tell me and I wasn't going to bother wasting my breath to ask. That was the way our family did things.

Which was one reason I was still so stunned that she had come here to talk to me about something she wanted help with. Something that had to do with talking our mother out of, well, pretty much anything. Which had never been something I ever tried to do.

Celestia or Andromeda had always tackled those types of situations. They were the ones Mom listened to. They were the ones whose advice she accepted. They were the ones who had made her proud in their professional lives and in their personal lives.

They both had impressive jobs. Andromeda was a banker, though he used the name Andrew there. I had always found it funny—and a bit weird—that it didn't actually seem to bother the woman who had, after all, named him. But, then, my opinion mattered little to her.

Celestia was an interior designer. Which I found ironic in so many ways. Since her job was just as much dependent on sales and creativity as mine was.

I guess the regular working hours makes all the difference.

Because it sure wasn't mentions in the press or interviews given in prestigious newspapers or on high rated talk shows that made any difference. Sure, Celestia had been featured in some architectural magazine and several that catered to designers, but my articles and interviews outnumbered hers ten to one.

Not that Mom... or Leda... or Celestia... or Andromeda... had ever mentioned a single one. Not one of them had told me they'd read any of the articles or watched the interviews. Not one of them had ever said they were proud of my achievement. Never had they said they were happy to see I was doing well in my chosen profession.

Why? Because my success had never made a bit of difference to them. I knew it. I'd known it for years.

And whatever it was that made the difference with everyone else, I had also figured out many, many years ago that I would never fit in with my family. None of them understood me. Even worse, they didn't seem to want to understand me, either.

But no matter how much I had wished that it could be different... that something would make them proud, I had eventually let go of it. I knew that their not understanding me would not stop me from writing. Because I didn't write for them. They didn't even bother reading any of my work.

Plus, I had an entirely different reason for writing now.

When I looked up again, the alien visitor was nowhere to be seen, though I was certain he must be there somewhere, preparing to do his job as muse.

So I sat down at the computer, opened a new document, and started writing.

chapter twelve

I wrote for hours.

I didn't stop for anything. The words flowed and I followed along... and the result may or may not have been specifically inspired. Though if it was, it definitely answered the question of whether or not my currently invisible alien visitor could read my mind.

He might be nowhere to be seen, but I had no doubt he was here somewhere... inspiring the story in whatever way he had helped inspire the first story I had written.

Likely the others since.

A small part of me wanted to be bothered by the idea that I had not come up with the ideas all on my own, but at the same time, I was absolutely freaking out over the idea that something I was writing about... an honest to goodness fantasy world—one that existed completely outside of everything scientific and logical as far as humans were concerned—was completely real... somewhere... out there in the universe.

And not just one.

If what he said was true, about there being others, there could be thousands of them. Even millions. And all with their own personal author here on Earth, and each reader doing their part to send some sort of reading magic off into the cosmos to support life on that planet.

The thought of so many authors out there in the world, doing just what I was doing, not even for all of the same reasons, was awe-inspiring. How many years had this mysterious mix of magic from stories being read fueling other worlds been going on?

Just as I was doing right now. Just by doing what I loved. What I would have done anyway, with or without inspiration.

Whatever the reason, whether his inspiration or my own determined—and slightly crazed—mindset, I wrote enough material for at least three of the special feature stories I had planned.

Thanks to my agent and his quick work, I now knew I could publish short stories on my author website and my social media, as long as they were under a certain word count.

They might not get the exact same level of readership that a new novel being released would get, but they would definitely, with over thirty thousand people following my blog, and at least twice that on social media, be read by a lot of people.

It couldn't be any worse than what's going on now with the sequels anyway...

I told myself it was better than doing nothing at all... it would have to be. I was doing the only thing I could do to help. That would have to be enough.

And though I was hesitant to assume I was a better writer than the ghost-writers the publisher was using, perhaps the readers would somehow make it known that they enjoyed the stories, and somehow make it possible for me to work something out with the publisher for one of the stories I had written to actually be published.

And hopefully that would be enough to help the people of Macus.

If it wasn't just wishful thinking...

The thought came to me out of nowhere — so strongly, I would have thought it somehow came from my strange alien visitor. Except for the fact that he had been nothing but determined in everything he had said and inspired and projected into my head.

He wanted this to work. So, surely he wouldn't think something so defeatist... would he?

Unless I'm rubbing off on him somehow...

That thought was so depressing, it pulled me completely out of the story world.

I sat back, stretching cramped muscles, reaching my hands to the ceiling above me and listening to all the strange little pops and clicks that my bones or my joints — or both — made. And I couldn't help but laugh, so completely distracted by all of the crazy sounds of my body coming out of the writer's hunch that was my normal posture from being so completely immersed in the story world.

My family really thinks this isn't work?

I had sat still in my chair, without moving or taking a

break to do more than click save in the document for hours. People in a normal job would have taken several breaks by now... to eat, to smoke, to do whatever they did in the fifteen minutes or half hour they needed in order to rest from their job.

I rarely needed a break from the thing that I loved doing, the thing I had never truly considered to be something so trivial as a job. To me it was a labor of love, a wish fulfillment, a dream come true.

It was all I had ever wanted to do.

I just wish my family could understand that... somehow.

I might have realized they wouldn't understand years earlier, but it didn't stop me from wishing it would change... that it could change.

Looking over at the picture on my desk of the family, Leda in the middle with the wide smile of a person who is completely oblivious to the true ways of the world, I couldn't help but think back to Leda's visit. Whatever was going on with her, it was clear that something needed to be said to Mom. Hopefully, she would know a bit more about what was going on with my sister.

With that in mind, I leaned back over the keyboard of my laptop, pulling up my e-mail account. I would send my mother a message. It would likely take her a few days

to get back to me, but at least I would find out what was
going on and I wouldn't have to actually talk to anyone
else.

I added in the usual pleasantries since Mom tended to
view e-mail as just a digital form of letter writing. Then I
mentioned that Leda had come by and had mentioned
that there was something going on with the house. Then I
closed with more useless chatter and sent the thing off,
satisfied that I had done something about it.

Once I had dispensed with the uncomfortable, if
necessary family message, I went about the business of
sending off a message to my usual freelance editor. I had
never told anyone about the wonderful woman I had
discovered online... under the most fortuitous
circumstances. But she had taken every single one of my
manuscripts and helped me turn them into pure gold.

She had been the first person to actually praise my
writing, to tell me how easy I was to work with, and how
little work she actually had to put into them.

At the time I had thought she might just be flattering
me, but when I'd asked her about it, she had assured me
it was no such thing. I could still remember the
incredulous tone in her voice.

*"Are you kidding me? Why would I ever tell you something like
that if it wasn't true? Don't you know how much more I could*

make if your work wasn't already in such excellent shape? Most people need two or three rounds with me. That's money in the bank, girl." And then she had laughed—and we'd gotten back to work.

It had taken me some time, but through lots of discreet inquiries in the few online author groups I belonged to, I had discovered that she must be telling the absolute truth.

Evidently, editors were much happier... most times... working with authors who needed intense editing because they made a lot more money with them than they did someone who just needed a bit of tweaking here and there —like apparently I did.

After that, I had made a point to keep sending her my manuscripts. Loyalty was something I was very unaccustomed to, given my family... and the city I had chosen to call home, and I was not about to take it for granted.

And it must have been the right choice because it had only taken about a week for Hill House to snap up the manuscript Steve had pitched them. They had signed me with a fat three book contract and Steve had made sure all the numbers were right where they should be.

It was one of the few advantages of the crappy deal I'd made with that first book. Since they didn't want anything further from me, I was free to work with other publishers.

And since their plans had been spoiled over the pen name, I got to use it, too. A point Hill House had been quick to capitalize on. They had wasted no time in launching a huge publicity campaign for that first book they'd bought.

Before it had even released, it was on multiple bestseller lists and the initial print run had sold out... even though they had told me themselves that they were not likely to sell out for at least a year.

Neither Hill House nor I had counted on just how many loyal readers would come over from the the series that first publishing house had put out.

Or else they just hadn't wanted to get their hopes up... and mine.

Regardless, the first book had sold quickly. And garnered stellar reviews. And Hill House had been quick to ask me what I wanted to work on next. They hadn't precisely given me the freedom to do whatever I wanted. Not that it would have mattered. Everything I wrote fit into some aspect of fantasy or other. It was just the way my mind worked.

That thought made me wonder something that had not occurred to me before—and gave me a question to ask of my strange alien visitor.

If he ever appears again, that is.

The possibility that he might not reappear, now that I was doing what he had asked, had not occurred to me until now. But I had to admit, since I was on track with my writing, it was possible that he would simply go back to doing what he was supposed to do.

I might never see him again...

For some reason, that thought depressed me. And I was more than a little relieved that I had stopped writing for the moment. I certainly wouldn't want to let this emotion leak into the writing. Stories that I was working to make as hopeful as possible.

I looked around the room, trying to figure out where he was... or if he was gone for the moment. He had to have been here earlier... hadn't he?

As much as I had written... as fast... and as easily as the words had flowed... That had been him... *hadn't it?*

I wished I could know for sure. I wished I could somehow see where he was in the room, like I had sort of seen through his human facade several different times.

I wanted to say something. To speak to him. To ask him if I was right... or wrong. But I had the sudden terrible thought that, if he was here, he would have known what I was thinking... which would mean either he couldn't — or wouldn't — show himself to me, now that he'd accomplished what he had shown himself to me to achieve.

Or else he was gone.

And the thought of that was... strangely... almost more than I could bear. My throat clogged on a thick, oppressive emotion that suddenly swamped me. My eyes were unexpectedly heavy with tears. My breathing hitched with unspent sobs. My chest was crushed by the weight of what it all could mean.

For a moment... just a moment... I told myself it was him. That he was here, and that he couldn't show himself for whatever reason. But that he was still trying to communicate with me in his way. In whatever way he could manage.

But there was nothing that spoke to that. No shift in the air. No answering thoughts in my mind. No imagery that told me I was on the right path. There was nothing I could hold onto that gave me any real answers as to whether or not I would ever again see the strange alien that had invaded my life.

And changed absolutely everything.

I trained my eyes at the chair where he had first appeared, looking at it through the bleary wash of tears that was breaking free without my permission. There was nothing there that I could see. And nothing about the space in it or around it gave me the impression that he was occupying it.

He was just gone.

There wasn't even anything left in the room to make me wonder. There was no feeling that anyone was watching me. No strange sense that the room had more than just one person in residence. It was just me now. I was all alone. And there was nothing that I could do.

I could call out. I could shout the house down. I could beg, plead, whine. But, at the end of the day, I couldn't make him come back. I couldn't make him appear.

The others who had come were pretty clear that he was never to have shown himself to me. He wasn't ever supposed to let me know he existed.

He had done so out of desperation. Which I completely understood. In his place, I liked to think I would have done essentially the same thing. I hoped I would have had the courage.

He'd put himself out there. Completely. Breaking the rules. Doing something so daring, so dangerous, so desperate. All to save a world in need. All for people he most likely didn't know any more than I did. People a thousand... or a million... worlds away. People he had no connection to other than what was required for him to do his job.

And it all could have gone so horribly wrong. It all could have been a tremendous waste of time. It could have ended up exposing the entire system—all of them.

What would that have done to the magic that was feeding the worlds out there? How would something like that have wrecked the system that fed magic to keep all of those worlds going.

Countless worlds. Countless lives. Destroyed.

I didn't want to think about that as even a teeny tiny remote possibility. I couldn't deal with what that could have meant. Not just for them, but for us. Certainly it would have affected us.

We could have lost our ability to dream, to fantasize, to dare to imagine... anything. And what if our world was also, in some way, dependent on that same magic? What if we needed it to survive?

It did not bear thinking of the disastrous consequences that could have... quite easily... resulted from his desperate—if also necessary—actions. The possibilities were too frightening to even consider.

So, I would have to find a way to go on without him... somehow. I had to believe. To trust that he would be there somewhere... somehow... doing what he was supposed to do, to help me do what I was supposed to do.

To write. To help. To save the world in need. My beloved Macus.

Squaring my shoulders, I made an effort to shake away the thoughts and go back to the business at hand, even more determined than ever to get things rolling as quickly as possible.

I kept my e-mail to Marie as vague as I could, thankful that she was not someone who understood the need for secrecy when it came to authors and their work. I knew she would get back to me soon, probably to ask why this story was so short... and probably why I was still hung up on a series I couldn't write any more installments for. She was one of the few people who knew that—and only because I trusted her completely.

Plus, she had asked me point blank about it, after she had edited two of the continuing stories I had worked on in hopes the publisher would want them... and then, when none of the other books they had published were mine.

She hadn't been fooled for a moment. A ghost-writer

herself, she knew how it worked and she was nearly as annoyed as I was over the whole thing when I explained to her what had been done.

She had lamented about not warning me... and then made sure to spend time telling me more about how it all worked, so I would be forewarned in the future.

I had assured her that it was no more her fault than mine. Who, but the devious publisher, could have seen any of it coming. Steve had even said he might not have figured it all out in time. Though he was also quick to point out that he would most likely never have allowed me to sign a deal that left me completely in the cold with royalties and a possibility to publish further books.

But since I had not signed with him until nearly a year after the deal was done — after the book had released and was making huge waves everywhere... and I had been caught having my own personal freak-out over the fact that my book was on bookshelves at an actual bookstore — all he'd been able to do was some damage control.

When a reporter had spotted me hugging the book to my chest, he had filmed it thinking it would be a good addition to his story about the success of the book from not only a debut author, but a complete unknown in every sense of the word. He could never have guessed he would end up blowing the whole mystery open and outing the author who had been kept a secret by the publisher on purpose... because they hadn't wanted anyone to know it was me.

Later, when he had watched the footage, and heard me saying to myself how I couldn't believe my book was actually published and in bookstores, he had done everything he could to track me down. But I had paid with cash for the things I had bought that day—and I didn't have a club card. And there was no one in the bookstore who knew me well enough at that time to know how to find me.

It had been a happy accident that had put the whole thing together for him. He had been in the bookstore cafe again about a week later when he saw me again. He had moved quickly, calling up a camera crew and approaching me very carefully, while I was still in the store.

And I, terrified that I would get into trouble with the publisher, had denied everything... until he'd shown me the footage on his phone.

Then, of course, I'd had no choice but to admit that it was all true. Though I was careful to keep my real name out of it—and anything about the whole ghost-writer part, certain those little tidbits would get me into trouble with the publisher.

After that, they'd had no choice but to admit I was the

author.

And, fortunately, I had gone in search of an agent. I was determined that I was not going to make another dumb choice where my work was concerned.

Steve had jumped at the chance to represent me. And he had worked out a deal for me to get paid for author appearances, have all of my travel covered for the tour they threw together—in just a few days—and to get expenses and other perks on top of everything else. Including free books, advance copies of upcoming books in the series, and the ability to use the pen name when I published other books elsewhere.

He'd told me there might be nothing I could do to change the original contract, but if they wanted to capitalize on the excitement that was building over unmasking the author for this series that was making an unprecedented splash absolutely everywhere, they would have to make it all worth my while.

And true to his word, he had made certain they did.

After hitting send on the last of my e-mails, I got up,

picked up my mug, which was still almost half full, and headed downstairs to get more coffee.

As I went through the house, I noticed that it was nearly dark outside. I had written what had been left of the day away already and I knew I could easily write for several more hours with more coffee to fuel me.

And have some food delivered.

That thought cheered me some. Living in New York definitely had its perks—and food delivery was one of them. Just within ten blocks of my house, there were at least a dozen different places I could get food without having to step one toe out the door.

With that in mind, I picked up my phone. Which rang just as I touched it. I jumped a little as I picked it up. And then I did a double take when I saw who was calling.

Already! She got my e-mail this fast? And she's calling me instead of just answering?

It was beyond unusual. This had never happened.

Clearly, something was up.

The voice that sounded when I pushed the button to answer told me there was more going on than even I had figured.

Mom sounded angry...

Even though she had never approved of my lifestyle... and my writing... and my relationship with my family, she had never sounded so indignant. What on earth was going on, anyway?

Before I could say anything, I was bombarded with the news I should have been prepared for... that once again, I had messed up, and poor Leda had done whatever she could to protect herself from mean old Aura.

After all, if I had a normal job, none of this would have happened. Right?

But honestly, how was I supposed to know that Leda, after I rightly guessed that she had come to me for money —again—would spin a huge lie about mom selling her home.

And of course, it was my fault that Leda lied about it, then left abruptly after I hurt her feelings.

When I finally pushed the button to end the call that felt like it was never going to end, I set down the phone. Then picked it right back up and turned it off.

Then I remembered that I had never gotten a chance to order food. But when I picked up the phone again, all I could do was cringe... just at the chance that one of my relatives might call again.

That was the way they worked. First my mother would call. Then my older brother. Then our other sister, the successful one, would call and pour on the guilt... or annoyance... or anger. Whatever emotion they were all trying to bombard me with.

At least they all work as a unit.

The thought left a bad taste in my mouth. Being thought of as the weak link was not the part of that unit I wanted.

With all of that rushing around in my head, I picked the phone back up, walked to the front door and dropped it in my purse. I would go out to dinner. And I would not turn the phone back on.

And that way, they could call the home phone all they wanted. I wouldn't have to turn it off or ignore it. I would not be there to hear it.

It was the perfect solution.

With as much of a smile as I could muster after such an exhausting day, I headed out the door.

chapter thirteen

When you start out on this amazing and unbelievable journey and then suddenly, without warning, without any real reason, and without any closure, that adventure changes... and all the time that you've already devoted to the project that might have driven anyone else insane with the sheer expectation attached... leaves you wondering...

Well, it doesn't actually end, but it certainly takes an unexpected, frightening, and—if I may say so—lonely turn.

What do you do? How do you just keep doing what you're doing? How do you forget all about the spectacular things you've learned, and go on with your life as usual?

Obviously you don't. You can't. Not really.

You realize that you just have to go on as best you can, trying to continue doing what you know must be done, to save innocent lives, to keep the magic flowing, to give some semblance of meaning to your life—and all of your hard work.

But your life will never be the same.

And you know that. Because you've been forever changed. You know things now that maybe you should never have known. But you know them. And you can't un-know them.

You just can't go on as if you don't know.

You have to find some way to carry on, to get the job done. Not to let down the people who are all counting on you, whether or not they know it.

And you have to find some way to make peace with the realization that you've gotten a glimpse—just a tiny peek—at a part of the world.

No, not the world. The universe. A real look at the universe. Something you never, even in your wildest imaginings, could have ever guessed existed.

Not only that, but you have to somehow take it all in stride, get the work done, and find a way to go back to your life. All the while, pretending that everything you've learned, all you know now... the amazing and astonishing discoveries that have forever altered your perception of life itself.

Yeah, you have to pretend they don't exist. Because they don't exist for anyone else. You must do it... pretend that you don't know what is behind the curtain.

Let me tell you, it is not an easy thing to do. Especially for a writer.

Authors have enough difficulty keeping all of their marvelous story ideas to themselves. With all of the amazing ideas we put down on paper. All of the things we learn about. The exciting things we know are coming. Book deals. Tours.

More stories to be released in beloved book series. It's hard enough to keep all of those secrets to themselves.

But then, to have to keep these new secrets. Things that would change the way people think about life as we know it.

To keep all of that to ourselves, too. It's a tall order. A very tall order. It could even be an impossible task.

A frightening realization is when an author knows more than any other... *like I do*.

When we know how things work outside our little world. When we know that our work affects more than just the people who edit, promote, print, sell, and read our books.

When an author knows precisely how far-reaching the effects his or her work actually has...

Well, we can't help but wonder what would happen to the order of things if we did spill those secrets? What would happen to all of the worlds that are being supported by magic? What would happen to the possibly alien creatures that are going about providing some sort of conduit of inspiration and guidance?

Most frightening of all... what if you actually tried to share that information with the world—and they didn't believe you? As one would obviously expect of fragile human beings.

We have such difficulty with true suspension of disbelief.

When reading a favorite fantasy or science fiction novel,

we can let go of it. We can pretend for awhile that what we are reading between those beautiful covers is actually possible, in some fantastical world that exists... somewhere... out there.

But when given actual evidence that such fantastic things actually do exist, can the human mind in general even begin to deal with the possibility?

Is seeing believing? Or is believing seeing?

What if it's neither? What if you have to believe, when there's no hope of ever actually seeing?

What if seeing would not guarantee actual belief?

What then?

I'm not convinced there is an answer. And, unfortunately, I don't know yet how I am going to deal with it.

When further writing proved to be a virtual impossibility, I decided the best thing to do would be to remove myself from the situation for a bit.

Mostly to tell me to get back to work... which would definitely be enough for me.

I must admit, it was nice that for just a little while, the most difficult decision I had to make was where to go. In a city like New York, time is not as much a factor on where you go as it would be in most cities.

There are bars on nearly every corner in the city... and more scattered out in the far flung neighborhoods.

Not mine, actually, but one was close enough to be an option.

However, I didn't want to just sit somewhere... alone... and drink. I wanted people around me, but not in a crazed, drunken, party atmosphere.

So, I went with the safe choice. I picked a favorite restaurant—*not* the one from that disastrous lunch. Another favorite in the city. One that was close enough to home that I could walk to in the daylight.

Then I decided not to walk. It didn't seem the safe thing to do. With darkness having completely descended upon the city, I did the smart thing. I called a cab.

When they picked me up, I gave the address to the driver, then I sat back and let my mind wander, working hard not to think about all that had happened over the last few days.

Unfortunately, I had very little luck.

My mind didn't seem to want to let me think about anything else.

Since I had not truly dealt with it all yet, it wasn't much of a surprise. Simply the fact that it had been a number of days since this had all began—not even a full week had passed—was mind boggling.

Then there was everything I had discovered.

If I was not, in fact, losing my mind. If everything I had witnessed over the last few days was actually real... had actually happened.

That too, was mind boggling.

Just the small amount of information I actually possessed still felt like too much to deal with.

To think that somewhere out there, only the aliens knew where, there was a world that was completely and entirely supported—and I still had so few details about that. It was not only boggling to my mind, but more than a little frightening.

He had never solidly confirmed it—not exactly. But I

got the definite impression that this was something that had been going on for some time. It was obviously somewhat organized. I had seen that first hand.

And I could guess about some of the other things I didn't know for certain, as well.

It wasn't hard to guess that these alien like creatures were all around us... like angels...

Or demons...

That thought sent an involuntary shiver through me.

It was one thing I had never considered during this entire crazy occurrence. The possibility that he was who he said he was... but perhaps not quite.

With what I had seen, I had accepted that he was not of this world. I had taken his abilities at face value. If I took for granted that I was not crazy... or imagining things... then he must be some sort of otherworldly being.

But what if he wasn't good... like I had just assumed?

What if the reason they hadn't stopped me from working, had more to do with causing a problem than stopping one?

What if all of those images he'd shown me would be the outcome of whatever they were doing — not the way to prevent them?

The thought was nearly too much for me.

Fortunately... or maybe unfortunately, the cab arrived at the restaurant just then.

I paid the driver. Added a tip. Got out of the cab. And headed inside, my heart suddenly heavy with worry and angst.

How would I know if it were true? I had just taken his word for it all. But how could I know? How could I check on it? There was no way to research something that no one else even knew existed.

If there was, an author would certainly have figured it out by now...

But none had. Or, at least, none that I knew about.

I told myself then and there that I would do some research when I got back to my house that night. If he was really gone, it would be the perfect opportunity.

This being one of my favorite restaurants in the city, the maître d' knew me. He actually knew me as myself *and* as the big deal New York Times Bestselling author I tried to keep quiet as often as possible when out and about in real life.

I'd never discovered if that had anything to do with the preferential treatment he made sure I received every time

I came in... or not, but I wasn't about to complain or tell him to treat me any differently.

And it wasn't as if he led me through the restaurant, calling out my name so all the other patrons knew I had arrived.

Which really might mean it just has more to do with my being here all the time.

That thought was oddly comforting. I had spent my life scratching and struggling for every little thing.

I hadn't gotten a scholarship for college, even though my grades had been just as good as friends and acquaintances I had known who had.

I had not lucked into one of the amazing rent controlled apartments like the one my dear friend from school still rented, because it was in a good enough part of the city for her to feel safe—and the rent was simply unbelievable. No matter how well her job was going, she insisted she was never giving up her apartment.

I had been fortunate to find an apartment close enough to the job I'd taken to make ends meet during school, and that I was able to stay with it, even though I'd had to share the apartment with two other people I'd known from school for three years.

Until the publisher had bought my story. And, even that had started out like so many other things in my life. They had wanted the story, but they hadn't wanted me.

Sometimes I wondered if that was really what had been behind my signing the deal at the time. It was more than I had expected, and I was so completely used to being shoved aside for others who didn't seem to be any better at something, or more qualified, than I was.

The sudden and intense fame I had accidentally acquired had been the sort of thing that I expected to see happen to other people. If someone had told me I would have such a thing happen to me, I would have called them a liar.

And then that reporter had unmasked me.

The craziest part of it was that I had gone to some pretty intense lengths to keep the secret. I had told no one in my family. I had told none of my friends. I had told neither of my roommates. I had just taken the money they'd paid me and made a big payment on my student loans, tucking away a small portion of it in my savings and then went back to my life.

When I had been standing at the New Release rack in the large chain bookstore near my apartment, holding my book that I had been certain, at the time, that no one would ever know was mine, I had squealed a little, but there'd been no one anywhere near me. And I had been so careful to keep my voice quiet.

Who could ever have guessed that a reporter would take a video with his phone, and then later, would watch it over and over until he knew exactly what I was saying? And even more, that he would stake out the bookstore until he saw me again, and then taking the time and initiative to call a news crew to come and ambush me.

It was one of those things that no one could ever have seen coming. And it was then that my life had really changed, in more than just the way that I actually got recognition for something I did.

With a flourish of his hand, the maître d' ushered me to my preferred table. I would have wondered if he had certain tables he kept empty during his favorite patrons usual visit times. But with me, that would have been impossible, unless he just never sat anyone else at the table.

Some part of me knew that was ridiculous, but the writer in me enjoyed it immensely. Mostly because it felt like the sort of thing that would happen in a book or a movie.

I slid into the booth and then sat there while they all went about the business of making me comfortable. Someone placed my napkin gently on my lap. The maître d' snapped his fingers for the sommelier, who presented a bottle of my usual wine with a flourish and a bow and the sharp snap of cloth.

I nodded and he was off, going through the ritual I always enjoyed watching. Every movement was so precise and exact, but more artful than a military show.

A waiter appeared to take my order, suggesting, as they always did, a meal that would compliment my choice of wine. I nodded again and then I was left alone to wait and drink my wine.

And time to remember...

Within a week of the story airing on television, I had an agent I trusted, a huge new deal with the publisher that had originally wanted nothing more to do with me, and the respect of thousands of readers all over the world.

And now I had the life I had always hoped for... mostly.

I had time to write—all the time I wanted. With the new deal Steve had negotiated for me, I'd spent the next six months on tour all around the country. I made enough from all of those appearances to pay my bills and save quite a lot of money toward getting my own place.

Since they had taken care of all my travel, my meals, my hotels, and any other expenses while traveling, I'd spent virtually nothing of my own the entire six months.

Then, Steve had negotiated a huge deal with Hill House Books while I had been on tour, which wasn't a surprise at all with my name and face splashed all over television and news for over six months.

Now I was a bestselling author of six books with a fancy house — even though two of the books weren't technically mine — a special table at my favorite restaurant, and the respect of thousands of people from all over the world.

And the biggest worry on my mind at the moment, was for an other worldly being who had told me the planet full of people I had only ever met in my head were very real and in desperate need of my help. Even more so, he had convinced me to find a way to write stories about them in order to keep them alive and well, and then he disappeared on me.

Which brought me full circle.

I worried that I might have imagined the whole thing... if I had been too quick to take him at his word. I was angry at all that he had put me through before just up and disappearing on me...

And I worried about him. About whether or not I would ever see him again, whether I would be able to go on without his inspiration.

Would the stories be the same? Would they have the same power? The same impact on the world? On whatever magic the world needed to go on spinning and surviving?

Would I be able to do it alone?

That anger bloomed again. How dare he make me question my talent? How dare he reveal all of these crazy things. Making me worry that I couldn't do the job all on my own.

And then just leave.

Just then, the waiter appeared with a lovely plate of food, compliments of the chef.

"A delightful little taste, just to stimulate the appetite..." He said it with an odd sort of grin, but no real hint of anything untoward. So, I thought little of it.

Mostly I went back to feeling sorry for myself. I sipped my wine. I ate the small, but generous appetizers slowly, enjoying them more than I'd expected to. But still wishing I was in a much better mood, so I could enjoy them with all of the enthusiasm they likely deserved.

My meal came. The waiter topped off my glass.

I ate slowly. Chewing and thinking and trying to figure out if I was more angry that he had come and upset my whole world... or that he'd done all that and then disappeared on me.

It was difficult to decide. One way, I was a petty, horrible, small-minded person who had no interest in how the world of fiction I lived in worked.

The other way, I was someone who had spent their entire life looking through a keyhole at the world. That keyhole had been widened to show me a large portion of what I had been missing. And then it had all been yanked away.

It didn't feel petty or childish to be angry... and annoyed... and hurt. It felt human. And I, at least, was human — and definitely prone to all-too human emotions.

Once the meal was finished, I could have made my excuses, asked for my check and left.

But sitting in a quiet corner booth, alone, not specifically drowning my sorrows, but at least giving them a good soaking, felt like just the place I wanted to be, even though it hadn't really helped my mood one bit.

I'd nearly finished the bottle of wine. I'd eaten enough of my meal to consider it finished. I'd even managed to do justice to the chocolate concoction the waiter had talked me into. I just hadn't come up with any answers, or ideas about how exactly to proceed.

I had enough material for several installments written. I'd sent it off to Marie and would have to wait for her to send it back before I could do much of anything else.

In the meantime, I would have to tackle the decision of whether or not to go on writing without my strange alien shadow.

It still rankled every time I thought about it... that I worried I couldn't do it without him.

I refused to believe that he was the source of my talent, of my dedication, even of my work ethic.

I should have just gone back in the office and written some more.

I felt it so strongly. And yet... feeling it and actually doing it are two very different things.

And writers are emotional creatures.

I learned a long time ago that creative people, especially writers, depend on our emotions a lot more than the average person. We soak up those emotions when we deal with things in everyday life. We store them. And then we pour them into our writing. Into our characters. Into the worlds that are populated by those characters.

Emotions are one of the biggest and most effective tools in an author's box of tricks.

Unfortunately, they are also one of the most crippling handicaps we possess.

When our emotions run away with us, authors cannot write. We cannot think. We cannot focus on the work before us. Even distraction isn't always a good solution. Because, all too often, distraction is done in by the very emotions we are trying to ignore.

So it was... on that particular late evening, after coming to such a disheartening realization, I sat alone, finishing up a bottle of wine and taking turns feeling sorry for myself and berating myself for not getting back to work.

Not that I could do much good with so much wine sloshing around in my system, keeping company with all the anguish and self-loathing.

And what should happen then, of course, but someone recognized me. Because that's just how these things work. When you've had a tureen of soup spilled in your lap... or you're very nearly under the table... someone will come along who expects to meet their hero.

And you have to find some way to give her to them.

And she's carrying my book, too.

Clearly, she was one of those people who carried books with her everywhere... or else she'd just bought it. Because when she walked up to the table, she held out the book I had actually written, the first book in the series.

Which either means she is a super, crazy fan... or else she just started reading the series.

Figuring out which would be the tough part. And I was not in a place at the moment to count on my faculties being exactly sharp.

"Oh my gosh. I know you're having dinner. And... I mean... I really don't want to impose... but..." She held out the book then, upside down to her, but in the perfect position for me to take it.

"Is there any way you would... consider..." She didn't finish, and I couldn't tell if it was because she was so embarrassed or if she was just hero worshipping and terrified to go on speaking.

I made myself smile and take the book, eternally grateful that I had gotten in the habit years before of carrying pens and sharpies with me absolutely everywhere.

And, fortune was again on my side. When I opened my disaster of a purse, a sharpie was sticking straight up, just waiting for me to pick it up.

So I took it, uncapped it, started to sign the book... and stopped, when she found her voice again.

"Oh, could you please sign it to Alexandria?"

Her voice was so quiet, I knew I would need to repeat the name and likely ask her to spell it. Since I wasn't exactly thinking clearly.

"You said Alexandria?" When she nodded, I added. "Is that the typical spelling, then?"

And, fortunately for me, she was one who did not take any chances with her name being spelled wrong. She spelled it out for me, speaking not much louder, but enough to hear her.

I wrote her name very carefully, adding a little note about hoping she enjoyed the book, and then signed my chicken scratch version of the pen name that still made me wonder if someone had just used some crazy random name generator online to come up with it.

When I handed the book back, she looked as if she wanted to say more, but fortunately, either nerves got the better of her or she couldn't think of what to say.

After several very long seconds, she mumbled a "thank you" and fled. I let out a breath of relief and motioned for my waiter.

When he arrived, however, I was in for another surprise. He didn't have my bill. Instead, he had a note from another customer in the restaurant who had apparently made arrangements with him to pay it.

The waiter handed it over with a secretive little smile, the expression of a co-conspirator. Which told me, whatever was going on, he knew more about it than he was going to tell me.

When I took the neatly folded piece of paper, the first thing I noticed was how fine it felt to the touch. This was obviously not a piece of paper the waiter had brought this person. It was clearly something they'd had with them.

Immediately my imagination went wild with that. Was it an agent who was trying to entice me away from Steve? Was it another of the strange aliens... perhaps apologizing for the way they had frightened me?

Or was it some reader who wanted to do something to get my attention, but was too timid to actually come and speak to me?

I told myself I was being silly. I knew my imagination was running away with itself, and part of it was likely due to my over drowning of what I still wasn't sure should be sorrows... or not. Since my alien could very well be back at any moment.

Stop being ridiculous. I told myself. *I will never know until I read the note.* I took a deep breath, unfolded the note, and started to read.

Good evening,

It was my pleasure to buy your dinner this evening. I would be delighted if you would allow me to do so on another evening, when we could enjoy the meal together.

It is a shame to watch such a beautiful woman dine alone. I would very much like to see that it does not happen again.

Yours

I found myself searching all around the restaurant, trying to deduce who had sent over the note.

Who could have written this?

Were they really serious? Or was it a joke? Would I be able to get the waiter to tell me who had given it to him? Were they still even in the restaurant?

Looking back down at the note, checking to see if I had actually read it correctly, I turned the words over and over in my head.

Could somebody be messing with me?

Could this be someone's idea of a prank? And, if so, why? What could be funny about doing such a thing?

Yours? Who signs a note like this with just "yours"?

It was the most ridiculous thing. If it was not a prank, just how was I supposed to answer? Especially since the waiter who had brought it to me had quickly disappeared and was nowhere to be found.

And the opening gave absolutely no clue as to whether he had just seen me and been attracted—or if he had recognized me and was hoping that his theatrics would give him a better chance at getting me to go out with him?

Neither option was any more or less obvious than the other. I looked at the note again for clues... anything that would tell me first, who the man was—and second, who he thought I was.

There was nothing in the words that even hinted at either answer. The greeting was too vague, and so was the close.

When I looked up again, searching for the missing waiter, there was a man standing in front of me, a very tall man. Judging from his clothes, I deduced that this was just the sort of man who would carry such fine note paper with him.

The breath I had been about to let out in a huff of annoyance, instead escaped in some sort of strange deflating balloon noise. And I actually felt my face fill with blood, likely turning my cheeks bright red in the process.

"Good evening." He completely ignored the strange noise I'd just made... and the beet color that had taken over my face.

"Would you care to accompany me to dinner?" He said the words so simply, but also elegantly, his voice clear and calm and strong.

I was becoming more convinced by the second that this must be some sort of joke... or, at the very least, a misunderstanding. What interest could this handsome and elegant man actually have in me?

I knew if it did turn out to be a joke that I would be playing right into the person's hands... but I was hesitant to pass up such an invitation. Especially if it had even the tiniest chance of being real.

My "yes" came out a little more squeaky than I would have liked, but he didn't seem to notice.

"Excellent." And he leaned forward a bit when he said it, in a little half bow.

It was at that point, I started to worry that perhaps it was not a prank... or a joke of some sort. This was real. And I had actually agreed to it. So, I was in the soup now...

"Would you be available this Friday at seven o'clock?"

I struggled for a moment to remember what day it was. One of the crazy things about being an author... the days all seemed to blur into one another. Steve had lamented that habit of mine more than once.

Before I could figure it out, I realized it really didn't matter. As far as I knew, I did not have any plans for Friday... whatever day it was. So I nodded, not wanting to chance another squeak.

He took my hand then... and kissed it.

And, as if that was not shocking enough, when he'd kissed my hand, he gave another little half bow and then he turned and walked away.

His... I don't know... driver, I suppose... came to the table about a minute later and asked me for my address.

I was tempted for a few seconds to give him my actual address... especially since I had no idea who he thought I was. But I never gave anyone my real address. Steve had given me that advice years before when my career took off.

So, I did what I always did. I gave him the address of a building that was several blocks from me, where I could wait for him, and pretend to be in the lobby by a happy coincidence when he arrived.

I tipped the doorman each month to let me do this. And he had always been really nice about it.

My house had no doorman, no lobby, no intercom system where someone had to press a button and wait for someone to answer. I just had a good old fashioned front door. It was what I had wanted when I'd started looking for a place to call my very own.

However, as the books had become more popular over the years, and fans had become more intense, I began to wonder about whether I should move to a building with a doorman.

Of course, then the question remained, would I give out my true address, and just trust the doorman — or would I keep doing what I was doing?

Once the other man had walked away, I decided it was time to go. I waited until I was reasonably sure he was safely out of sight, before sliding out of the booth and heading for the door.

I was out of the restaurant before it occurred to me that I had agreed to a date with a man whose name I still did not know.

And, on top of that, I had absolutely no idea who he thought I was.

I was not even a little tempted to write when I returned home, which I felt confirmed my suspicions quite nicely. If there had been anyone there who was trying to inspire me to write, I would have felt the need to go and write.

But I didn't.

I also knew that I would not hear back from Marie until at least the next day... or possibly longer if she was busy.

So, the only logical thing to do was crawl into bed and sleep off the depression that had done everything to run me over during the course of the evening.

Everything will look better in the morning.

I told myself the lie, but I knew it was only intended to make me feel better, so it did little good. Fortunately the liter and a half of wine in my system had me dropping off to sleep fairly quickly.

It was the next morning, fortified with a brisk shower and several cups of coffee, when I was working hard to keep up a hopeful attitude, that I finally ventured back into the office.

I told myself it didn't mean anything that I felt no rush of inspiration when I went in. But nevertheless I began to worry a bit.

Then a thought occurred to me. What would I do if my strange alien visitor never again showed himself to me... whether it was due to his having accomplished his mission or simply that he was no longer able or allowed to.

What would I do then?

I stopped myself from calling out, already feeling pretty silly about the whole nonsense of missing someone that I wasn't sure even existed. Though... to be completely fair, I wasn't entirely convinced my imagination was that exceptional... to come up with such a fantastical story.

I sat down at the computer, looked around the room and debated with myself again about whether or not it would do the slightest bit of good to call out, then decided that I was doing no one any good just sitting there.

If he's going to come back, he will... if he exists. And hopefully when I need him most.

I took some comfort in the fact that I had made such a successful beginning the day before. I had a lot of material to work with, a lot of directions I could take the story.

I would just have to work with what I had until he came back.

If he comes back...

I shut that thought down as quickly as it came. Squaring my shoulders and blowing out a quick breath, I gave myself a little shake, both physically and mentally.

I had written plenty of stories, all by myself, never knowing anything about this crazy little world that was not meant to be seen. I could do it again. I did not need some weird alien to inspire me or push me or whatever it was he did.

These were my stories, my ideas, my passion—and I was not about to let one little roadblock take them away from me.

With that firmly in mind, I opened the laptop and went

into the document I'd last been working in.

However, before I could type a single word, the notification for an incoming e-mail caught my attention. First, because I had forgotten to turn off the laptop's wi-fi... which only ever proved a distraction when I was trying to write. Second, because the name that showed was Marie's.

She's already getting back to me?

That worried me more than a little. Was there a problem? Did she hate what I'd sent her?

Before I could get too far into the crazy making world of what-ifs, I clicked to open the message.

It didn't take long at all to see what the problem was.


```
Hey Aura,

I was looking over what you sent me. First
of all, WOW! What fun this project sounds
like. Your fans are going to go nuts!

Second, while I love what I've read so
far, are you planning for this to be a
back-story thing or were you trying to keep
up with where the story world is at the
moment?
```

I don't know if they've sent you the next book that's scheduled for release in the series... and you just haven't found time to read it... or if they haven't sent it to you yet?

I have a friend who works for that publisher, and she knows I know you, so she sent me the next manuscript to look over.

Firstly, she's very concerned with where they've taken your story world... and obviously she doesn't know it's not you writing it. Secondly, she was trying to figure out what to say to the publisher when she turns this book back into them.

She is very concerned that the fans are going to hate this story.

I'm stalling. I'm sorry. I hate to be the one to tell you this, Aura. But they've wrecked your beautiful world. I mean really wrecked it. It's a complete and total tear down. I have no idea where they're going with all of this, but I'm beginning to think they're trying to just end the series or something.

It's terrible.

I'm attaching the document, so you can take a look at it for yourself.

Maybe they haven't sent it to you and this is why. They have to know you'll be upset over this. I know I'd be ticked off.

Anyway, just letting you know what's going on. I'm going to go over what you sent me. The way you've written it so far, it could easily be back story.

But if you're going to fit in with where the story is going, you might need to do some tweaking... or else write something else entirely.

Just wanted to give you a heads up.

Later!

Marie

I sat back with a thud.

There were no words for the shock that coursed through me. It took several minutes for me to compose myself enough to read over the e-mail again, hoping against hope that I'd misunderstood... somehow.

But no. It was all there. Everything I had thought I'd read was exactly as I remembered it. They had destroyed my beautiful world.

This explains those images.

He had known all along. Why hadn't he told me?

Better yet, why didn't the publisher's rep tell me at that disastrous lunch?

She had to have known. They would not have sent her to a meeting like that without giving her a heads up on where the series was—and where it was going.

No wonder they hadn't been interested in my story. They were trying to kill my series.

Well, we'll just see about that.

Without opening the document Marie had attached, I opened a new document, turned off my wi-fi connection, and got down to writing.

If they thought they could kill off my world, they would have another think coming...

chapter fifteen

It's one thing to discover that everything you thought you knew is wrong. It's entirely another to discover that your life's work has been more or less destroyed, by someone who clearly cared nothing for the world you hold so dear to your heart.

And when you add the insult that the publisher refuses to even look at another of your stories, but they'll pay some hack to destroy your beloved world in such a way...

Well, it's enough to drive you to drink.

Or actually, in my case, it's enough to drive you to do something about it—especially given how much I had drank the evening before.

Which is exactly what I did when I put down the travesty that was the fourth installment of the series I was very tempted to find some way to distance myself from.

I sat down at the laptop and wrote.

I wrote something completely different from what I had sent Marie. I wrote something that would come after the travesty, something that would hopefully keep my readers from rushing to the bookstores and demanding their money back.

I had pretty much planned on posting the stories I'd sent Marie just before the next book released anyway... as a sort of back story bonus.

But these new stories would come later. These would be my answer to what the publisher and their ghost writer was trying to do to my precious fantasy world.

These stories could—if the readers reacted the way I expected them to—either make the publisher rethink their terrible idea... to destroy my beautiful fantasy world, or maybe even make them decide they might want to take another of my stories after all and publish it.

If what Maria said was true... And, from what I had read, it certainly felt true. The readers were going to hate this next installment, the book I would have to pretend I had written. The book I would have to sit at signings and conferences and interviews and defend... for months or maybe even years to come.

It felt almost as if they were trying to hurt me.

They were certainly doing everything they could to hurt the people of the world I had brought to life. On the page at least.

I had already written well into the night before, falling into bed at a ridiculously early hour... yet again. Only when I had awoken and refueled with coffee, had I opened the file Marie had attached to her e-mail, knowing I could not put it off forever—and that I would have to match up my own stories to where the publisher was going with their next release.

This was not at all what I had envisioned when I had begun reading the obviously unedited pages. I had laughed to myself about how much more work this manuscript needed and how Marie might wish she had the chance to bill for all of the extra work it would take to get it into shape.

And then I had been distracted by the story.

The story that was almost exactly the opposite of what the series had begun with, taking a wonderful fantasy world that, yes, had seen strife and difficulties... but what world hadn't?

But this... this war torn and decimated world bore no resemblance to the one in my mind.

Who could have done such a thing? Who would have done such a thing?

And why did the publisher not see that this was such an intense deviation from the direction that all three books in the series so far, had taken?

How did they not think the readers would notice? Who had convinced them that this was a good idea? For my world? For this wonderful series?

And why didn't someone warn me... well before now?

There were no answers of course. I didn't expect any, and I knew there was no sense really... to any of it. It wasn't as if this move made any more sense than their continued refusal to consider one of my submissions for the series I had, after all, made such a big hit to begin with.

There was really only one option left; to do my part and hope it would be enough.

Perhaps if I gave the readers enough of my own material to read, it would somehow balance out the damage the other books in the series were doing.

There was nothing else I could do.

I wrote up a storm. I wrote about a world that was shattered and broken and destroyed. A people who were filled with hopelessness and despair. A people who were preparing themselves... for the time when they could stand up and fight again... and get things back to where they needed to be. For themselves. For their children. For their people.

The story world swallowed me whole. In a way it had not for months. If I had been able to stop, I might have wondered about my strange alien visitor. Whether he was somewhere close by, invisible, but still inspiring the words that were quite simply pouring from my fingers on to the digital page. Or if perhaps, I was actually doing this all on my own...

If I never saw him again, would that answer the question for me — or would I always wonder? Again, there were no answers.

Had I thought to, I might have taken the time to eat... or drink... or visit the bathroom.

But the story world had such a grip on me, I felt nothing

aside from the cold despair that filled the air around me. Air that was actually thousands or maybe millions of light years away from where I sat. But surrounding me nonetheless.

I felt hunger, but it was not my own. And I used it to drive the desperation of the young protagonist I had never even met before I had sat down at the keyboard only minutes... or had it been hours... earlier?

The hopelessness swamped me, wringing from me even more emotion than I knew I was capable of.

I was this young waif, desperate, alone, starved, terrified of everyone and everything around me. The ache for my family was heart-wrenching, choking me with such anguish and despair, I felt as if I could not possibly survive it.

There was no relief from the cold or hunger, no hope of shelter or care, no break from the fear that I could die at any moment... or be subjected to unthinkable punishment or torture.

It was agonizing. It was horrifying. It was gripping.

It held me so firmly in my seat, I couldn't have moved if the building had been on fire.

It might have been hours or even days before the furor finally released me enough to allow things outside of my little fantasy world to intrude.

I sat back and looked around the room.

If my strange alien visitor was there somewhere, there was no evidence of him. I had no idea if he had been inspiring what I had just written... or not.

Worrying as I had been that I might never see him again, whether he stuck around to inspire my work or not, I should have been more upset—or at least more curious—but I was on too much of an excitement high to let it get me down at the moment.

I had done something... finally... about the feelings that had been building since I had signed that horrible contract with a publisher who had done me wrong... And was still doing me wrong even now.

It hadn't taken very long for me to realize how I felt about the sneaky and underhanded way they'd gotten my story. And even less time to be really angry about it.

Pretty much the time it had taken for me to discover what they had done. How they had taken advantage of the situation. Of me—and my lack of knowledge in how things were done in the publishing world.

I had learned that lesson the hard way.

At some point after Steve had worked his agent magic, gotten me a surprising number of perks... though still—none of the royalties... I had convinced myself that I wasn't angry anymore, that I was perfectly content with the way things had turned out.

But, sitting at my desk, reading the awful novel they had lined up to release next, had shown me I was not content. I was not over it. I was not in a good place at all about it.

And the memory of that horrible lunch with the publisher's rep had just rubbed salt in an already nasty wound.

At the time, I hadn't seen it. Likely because I had been dealing with issues much larger than getting a book published. And then, of course, I had been dealing with the stress and pressure to figure out a way around the publisher.

And then the incredibly tense visit from even more aliens.

It was no wonder I had pushed all of it to the side and ignored what had been there for a very long time.

But now I was letting it go. I was pouring it into the writing. I was putting those emotions and that tension and stress and anger into something that would hopefully help more than just me.

Hopefully, it would also help the people of Macus.

There was also the added bonus that, by the time I would be off touring for the horrible book, I would have already posted several of my back-stories online, the ones that would have to be set before this latest atrocity.

I had faith that Maria would have them back to me in time. She worked quickly. We had worked together now on several projects, so I had complete faith in her... so much more than I had in the publisher—or anyone else involved with this blatant attempt to corrupt the beautiful story I had created.

At least I had the satisfaction of knowing, not long after the upcoming book's release, I would also be able to post these new stories. Shine a little light into the darkness they seemed determined to drown my world in.

Maria would work her magic with them as well—and I would have something to offer my readers aside from the dark, hopeless, mess that was beginning to make me wonder about whatever was actually going on with the people of Macus.

If the situation there was dire enough for the strange alien visitor to make himself known to me, going against all of their rules in his desperation, there must be more to the situation than he had let me in on.

Something was causing the world to be in danger, something I was just beginning to truly worry... and wonder about.

This bizarre situation had blinded me to my normal curiosity in so many ways. Yes, I had asked questions. But... they were the questions of someone who has just been shocked by an event so momentous, it shakes the very foundations of their existence.

Now that I was beginning to get used to the idea... now that I was delving back into my beloved fantasy world, I was starting to see things differently again. My curiosity was coming back to life, blooming, blossoming, pushing me to poke into corners and look beyond what was obvious—like I had not really done in years.

It was surprisingly refreshing.

Who could have suspected that having my world turned upside down and split apart could also have managed to tear down the walls I had not even realized I'd built, around my heart and my talent...

I had been hiding. Playing it safe. All these years.

And now that those walls were crumbling, I felt a freedom I hadn't felt since the beginning of my writing career.

No publisher was going to stop me from telling my stories to the world. No silly contract was going to keep the truth of how amazing a world Macus was. No boundaries could hold this light within.

With a smile and a much lightened heart, I attached the new files to an e-mail for Marie and dashed off a little note.

I thanked her for letting me in on what was going on with the new book in the series. I let her know I had read the manuscript and the new story I was attaching was my answer to it.

I also let her know there would be more forthcoming... soon.

Now I just had to wait for her to finish working on what I had sent her to begin with. Then I could share it with my fans and readers.

I couldn't guarantee how many would read it. But I hoped that enough of them would read the first stories...

before the next book came out... and watch for more before deciding that they were not interested in the series anymore—after what was certainly going to be a fiasco.

With the E-mail sent, and an entirely new hunger making itself known, I went in search of food... and coffee. I would need fuel if I intended to keep going.

And... oddly, I did feel like writing more.

Whether it was inspirations' effect or not, I was in the mood to write. And something told me there was a pretty good chance another late night was in my future as well.

Not like that's anything new. And I laughed as I took the last few steps two at a time. It was amazing to find that I felt like laughing for the first time in days. It was absolutely incredible how much lighter I was feeling.

Not only was I on a writing high. The burden I hadn't even known I was carrying, one that had been weighing me down for years, had evaporated like rubbing alcohol.

Downstairs, I picked up the phone to order food. Not wanting to take the time to cook... or even look through my cabinets to see if I had enough food to cook. Especially since I couldn't remember the last time I had shopped.

I hadn't even shopped to replace the coffee pot I had smashed the morning of that horrible lunch meeting. I had ordered a replacement online.

I'd been using the old, teeny coffee maker that I'd brought with me from the old apartment—the one I had only kept as a backup. Something I was incredibly grateful for now.

When food had been ordered, I turned to that coffee maker. First I had to empty the old, cold coffee and wash the pot out. Then I went about the business of making a new, full pot, which might or might not be enough to get me through the next phase of my writing.

While I waited for the coffee to brew and the food to be delivered, I leaned against the counter and let my mind wander a bit.

For some inexplicable reason, my mind wandered to the most unusual, unpredictable place it could have— especially since I had been so totally immersed in a fantasy world for the last day at least...

Family.

I couldn't help but think of that strange visit from my sister... How many days ago had it been now? Two... Three? Who could remember, with so many late nights and strange aliens showing up to scare the life right out of me?

And then... the even stranger call from our mother. She'd had no more idea than I what Leda had been after when she'd let herself into my house, but she was more than a little annoyed that she would have to deal with her youngest daughter now that I had evidently alienated her —the irony of her phrasing had not been lost on me in the moment, even as stressed out as I had been—to the point that she would apparently not even use my name when speaking to others in the family.

It was nothing new. Leda would get some strange idea into her head and then do her best to drag the entire family along with her as she "invested" in what she was certain would make her and anyone else involved rich beyond belief in no time flat.

Typically, one had to walk a fine line with her, playing a game of vague questions and gentle queries until she came to the point of actually asking for what she wanted —although it rarely felt like asking, more like some ridiculous shakedown, one that had to be done on her terms.

The alternative being that drama ensued for months, with her lamenting to everyone else in the family that she was being mistreated by the errant member who had lost patience with her childish begging and refusal to take any sort of adult responsibility for herself.

Having been on the receiving end of more than one of her tirades—and far more than my fair share of being the relative she was actively complaining about, I knew all too well how long it would be before everything went away.

Which was one reason I had switched off the phone after ordering food. And, it was the reason I had set the landline to go straight to voicemail.

It was just easier.

chapter sixteen

The day passed much as I expected it to, especially with all phones off and email being ignored.

I had ordered in enough food to feed myself for days. And, fortunately, I had enough coffee on hand to fill a small swimming pool.

So, I had taken advantage of the temporary absence of distraction and I had continued to write. I had sat at the computer until the screen blurred and the fingers tapping the keys were nearly numb.

Having never gotten completely dressed, falling into bed fully clothed was no problem. The lounge wear I'd shrugged on after my shower was comfy enough to sleep in—and no one was around to notice wrinkles.

Unless he's around here somewhere and just refuses to show his face.

The thought of my missing alien visitor had barely crossed my mind all day as well, so immersed had I been in the story world all day.

It was thrilling to know that I had enough material for absolutely months of blog posts—and that was if I posted once a week. Even with needing a lot of readers, it would not do to post more often than that. There had to be some element of anticipation or the readers would quickly lose interest.

My mind was plotting out the first blog post, the most important one... the big introduction, as sleep claimed me. When my eyes opened the next morning, my mind immediately returned to that first blog post.

Though... I was fairly certain there had been some rather strange dreams in between closing my eyes and opening them.

Not that there was any evidence of said dreams. Just a slight niggling sensation somewhere in the back of my mind that told me I had forgotten something.

Before I could wonder too much about it, another niggling sensation took over my attention. A large part of the food that had been ordered in had been Chinese take-out that New York was well-known for.

However, the place I usually ordered from had been closed when I called, so I had braved a new place—one that had left one of their menus attached to my doorknob with a rubber band at some point in the last month.

Note to self: no more ordering in from somewhere unknown without at least checking out the reviews online.

To say I dragged myself out of bed would have been an understatement. The combination of writing nearly until the sun was up—and chicken that was beginning to make it's presence known practically had me crawling toward the bathroom.

There had been no wine consumed the entire evening. I'd been doing too much writing for that. So, it was obvious that feeling like death warmed over must be due to some combination of a lack of sleep and the somewhat questionable meal I had ordered in—though it had looked, smelled and tasted fine at the time.

Clearly, it had not been fine. The nausea that swept over me with every step told the story.

Disappointment was almost as difficult to swallow as the taste in my throat that made me want to curl up with the porcelain centerpiece of my bathroom and let everything go.

I had a busy day planned. More writing had been planned—and then editing, before sending the next batch of stories that had taken hold of me off to Marie.

I'd only stopped the night before—or rather earlier that morning—because my entire body had begun to protest the hour and demanded sleep.

Since that was nothing new for me, I figured the chicken must have also had something to do with it.

Or else the culmination of the emotional roller coaster I had only begun to realize I had been on for years, and the pouring out of all that emotion, was also to blame.

Whatever the culprit, I had too much to do that day to just lie in bed.

When the chime announcing someone at the front door sounded, the thought occurred to me that I could pretend I was not at home, cancel the cab I'd called, call the doorman at my safety pickup building and ask him to cover for me, and just go back to bed.

I felt pretty confident that Henry would cover for me. He was a good guy. He'd been a fan of mine from the beginning apparently, and had been completely blown away when I had asked if I could use his building as a cover.

He'd also insisted he did not need anything other than a little conversation now and then... and autographs in each new book that was released to do this little thing for me.

But I had insisted, too. I wrote it off as a business expense anyway. And I certainly didn't ever want to feel like I was taking advantage of a fan... Especially such a nice one.

He was a super nice fan. And a nice man, too. He was always thrilled when I showed up with each new book, before it was available in stores, autographed and personalized with a little note just for him. We had some of the best conversations about the books, about life in general, about family and friends and New York.

Well... maybe not so much with the next one.

I thought about it bitterly. Actually, the worst part of it was that he would be excited when I showed up with the next book... just not the one after that. It felt like the worst sort of betrayal.

Especially since he was someone I considered more than just a fan. He was more of a friend.

A friend I knew would cover for me if I asked.

For about two seconds, I was really tempted. My writing had not been going well all day. I had a massive headache. And I was still regretting the chicken I'd ordered the night before.

But I had agreed to attend the dinner date with the still quite mysterious man who had bought my dinner several evenings before, and I had to admit that I was more than a little intrigued.

First, about why he had asked me. Then about why he'd decided rather arbitrarily to buy my dinner. And about whether or not he knew who I was.

There had been no hint in his behavior the other night. And he had never said my name. In my diminished capacity, I hadn't noticed anything that would have told me one way or the other.

Now I had to wonder. And wondering had made

dressing for the evening difficult. He had said we were attending a benefit. Black tie. Since I had been a bit dressed up for dinner, I had to assume he thought I was wealthy enough.

But that still did not tell me whether he had asked *me*, dressed up and obviously wealthy enough not to embarrass him at a society benefit... or *me*, best selling and award winning author, with no consideration beyond bragging rights and having such a well-known personality on his arm at a big to-do.

"Hopefully, time will tell." I muttered under my breath, just as I made the decision to go, pulling open the front door before I could change my mind.

Henry took one look at me when I stepped from the cab and cringed—which did not make me feel any better about the hour I had spent on my make-up and outfit.

"Are you sure you're up to this?" His voice told me he didn't think the answer would be yes.

When I had first mentioned the invitation to him, he had

been excited, caught up right with me in wondering if the mystery man had recognized me or not.

Henry was convinced that he had not recognized me, and that he was simply interested in me—romantically, imagining a happily ever after for one of his favorite authors.

It was sweet, but naive. Not something so unexpected from someone who had been happily married for more than half his life, with two beautiful girls, several grandchildren, and a large family of people who were pretty much all as blissfully happy as he was.

He had no idea of my track record with men. It wasn't something I had shared with him... mostly because it was too embarrassing. Dating had never been something I was terribly good at. The people I was most comfortable with were fictional.

Beyond that, I had a small group of good friends, some of whom were aware of my real identity—like Marie, some of whom were not—like Henry. None of them were what I would call a romantic interest... certainly not Henry, who was quite happily married and constantly showing off pictures of his newest grandchild.

In high school, I had always been hiding in a book, either a textbook or a novel. Noticing boys had been about as low on my interest list as acquiring a zit.

College had been much the same story. Having moved to New York for school, a strong determination not to fail had held my interest on my studies and away from romance.

Working two jobs; waitressing and writing, outside of school hadn't helped either.

Any free time I had outside of my waitressing job and full load of classes was quickly gobbled up by the characters and stories in my head, clamoring to get out.

After being discovered as the mysterious new author, I'd been asked out on more than a few dates. But each one had been worse than the last, because they weren't actually interested in dating me. It didn't take long to discover that they all had an ulterior motive. Every single one of them had been after something; fame, fortune or a stepping stone to my publisher.

There was no use explaining that the publisher responsible for my best-selling series was not going to help out any of my friends... not that Steve would have let me send anyone else's manuscript to them anyway.

Hill House might have been excited for me to bring them a new author or two—if any of the manuscripts that found their way into my hands had been good enough to pass on.

Sadly, they were all at least as bad as the dates that went along with them... some worse.

And that was saying something.

"So, is it nerves or another of your crazy late nights?" Henry's question pulled me out of my self-pitying reverie with a start.

Trust him to see right through my carefully applied makeup.

"Well, it's not nerves." I laughed a little as I said it, trying to sound nonchalant, but probably sounding standoffish.

Oh well... It was only Henry. He would understand, at least.

"I'm pretty sure it's food poisoning."

Henry whistled a breath through his teeth. "And you're still going tonight? He must be good looking." He laughed at his own joke.

I was shaking my head before I responded. "It's not his looks. It's the mystery. I'm simply intrigued."

"Sure. We'll call it that." He was laughing at me again, not out loud, but with his tone and the look in his eyes.

I shrugged. I didn't have anything to prove. Besides which, I felt like crap. I just wanted to get the mystery solved and get the night over with.

"Think what you want. I know why I'm here." I headed for the elevator bank, knowing it made it that much more convincing when I walked over from them... as if I had just come down.

Looking at my watch, I took a chance that he would be on time at least—and sunk into the cushions of the bench by the main elevator.

It was mostly obscured from the front door, unless someone thought to look into the large mirror over Henry's desk—which was the trick I used to see whether or not the person I was waiting on had arrived or if it was just someone who lived in the building coming home. I would check it out whenever I heard traffic sounds.

So far, no one had No one had noticed yet exactly where I'd come from... or that I was watching for them in the mirror's reflection—or, if they had, none of them had thought to mention it.

Not that I cared either way. Especially tonight, with an unsettled stomach and too little sleep, it was all I could do to hold my head up while I waited, much less dwell on whether or not someone who was no longer a part of my life had noticed a tiny detail like whether or not I had actually walked out of the elevator a second or two before they turned the corner.

chapter seventeen

It was not a driver who walked into the spacious lobby of what I had come to think of as Henry's building.

It was the man himself.

That shocking fact had me so momentarily distracted that I nearly forgot where I was sitting—and that I was supposed to be making a show of getting off the elevators... coming to meet him—the fortuitous meeting in the lobby, the chance encounter I had faked dozens of times, with Henry looking on.

Scrambling up from the bench, gathering my bag and keys and phone, taking a deep breath, I turned just as a deep, masculine voice sounded from my left... well, from my left before I had turned. Now, it was pretty much directly in front of me.

"Ah. Punctual as well. How wonderfully unexpected."

I looked up. Even in heels, I was several inches shorter than him. He was wearing a warm smile, but there was a twinkle in his eyes that told me either he was making fun or there was something he was not saying.

I wanted to ask... especially since curiosity was as natural to an author as breathing. However, there were still too many other questions I had about this whole interaction, to be so familiar right away.

And then I thought about what he had said—and, not at all true to character, a clever quip tripped off my tongue before I even had time to think about what I was saying.

"Eh... I had nothing better to do." I even added a slight shrug at the end for effect.

For a full ten seconds, though it felt much longer than that, he stood there, quietly. Just looking at me as I looked at him. The two of us locked in a silent staring contest.

Then he smiled.

"Well, then. I suppose I should feel quite the fortuitous fellow." And then he held out his arm and said "Shall we?"

Surprise had me nearly fumbling. There was nothing forced or annoying about his smile, so that threw me off balance a little. Obviously, he had gotten the joke. Was it possible I had finally found someone who could actually appreciate my odd sense of humor?

And maybe... just maybe, his own sense of humor was just a little devious as well.

Wouldn't that make for an interesting turn of events...

Whatever the case, I was only more intrigued. So, I took a second to drop my keys into the small bag I'd brought along and tucked my arm around his.

As we passed Henry, he winked at me, obviously certain he had been correct all along. "Have a wonderful evening, you two."

I smiled back, thinking that a wonderful night just might not be such a tall order after all.

It wasn't until we were pulling away from the curb that I realized my stomach had settled a bit—which told me that more of my queasiness than I'd realized must have been due to nerves. It made sense, with my past—and with not knowing who this man was, what he knew or didn't know about me... and what he was after with me.

Somehow, his demeanor had put me at ease enough that my stomach settled—and I found that I was actually looking forward to the evening.

I turned to speak, just as he did.

"I must tell you how exceptional you look this evening."

His comment certainly caught me off guard. Stomach issues aside, my lack of sleep had made eye makeup the priority of my beauty routine. How could any of that figure into exceptional?

I had no idea, but he went on before I could think of a proper response anyway.

"I do apologize for not mentioning it before. You quite took me by surprise."

And again... before I could stop myself, a quip tripped past my lips flippantly. "Because I was actually ready on time?"

Shockingly, he laughed—not a laugh that said he didn't know what to say or a laugh that told me he was annoyed and just covering until he could come up with an appropriate response to my smart remark, but a genuine laugh that lit up his whole face.

It was several seconds before he finished laughing and spoke again. "Actually, that is not at all what I meant. However, you make an excellent point." And he laughed again.

I relaxed a little more. This was turning into a wonderful evening—not just a good one—and certainly not another one for my list of worst dates ever.

We made small talk the rest of the ride, which was nice, but a teeny bit frustrating. Absolutely nothing that was said told me who he thought I was and he never once said my name... or his.

By the time we arrived at the benefit, my nerves were back, turning the butterflies in my stomach into fat, hopping frogs. The door opened—and a young man in a crisp, black suit reached for my hand to help me out of the car.

This was the moment of truth. Before I had even straightened completely, reporters were calling my name —my fake name, throwing out questions. Photographers were snapping my picture. Once he stepped out, his expression would tell me what I needed to know. I hoped so, anyway.

I turned to watch him step out—and was surprised again... and confused. The name still being yelled out behind me was clearly no surprise to him, but there was something in the tightening of his lips that told me he wasn't entirely happy about it.

He said nothing, just stepped out, took my hand, tucked it around his arm and headed for the door, ignoring every reporter on the way in with a skill I was instantly jealous of. It wasn't until we were in the doors that I realized I had ignored them all too—whether I'd meant to or not.

I was simply too perplexed by his demeanor. Was he annoyed at all the attention I got as we walked in? Was he only looking like my name didn't surprise him? Had he thought I was someone else and was now bothered to find out that I was someone famous?

"Do they hound you like that everywhere you go?" His question took me by surprise, as did his voice. He was speaking softly, but with an undertone of anger that felt... not out of place exactly, but more forceful than I would have expected for what was a normal occurrence for me. It took me a second to answer.

"Only at something like this. Mostly I get recognized by readers... and by fans." After a second I added, "I'm lucky enough not to be famous enough to be recognized constantly by reporters, unless it's someplace like this, where they're expecting big names."

"It's so intrusive though. How do you deal with it all?"

I looked up at him, expecting to see regret along with the obvious distaste in his voice. There was neither in his expression. His expression looked more like concern... and maybe even fear or worry.

Worry... for me? That was a new one.

I couldn't remember anyone being worried for me—or about me—in years. Even my agent, he worried only about getting a good deal for me because he wanted his percentage to be as large as possible.

Before I had a chance to ask him about it, we were stopped—not by someone who recognized me, but by someone who knew him... which was very interesting, but gave me little actual insight into the man I was even more confused about than I had been before he had so mysteriously asked me out.

At least I seemed to have my answer about who he had thought he was asking out on a date. He didn't hesitate one bit when he introduced me—as C.W. Starr. Not surprising. It made sense that an internationally Bestselling author from New York City would be so much more interesting than boring ol' Aura Jenson from nowheresville, Maryland.

It only took about two seconds for me to figure out that neither one of them had ever even picked up a copy of my books. But, they'd clearly read enough reviews of those books in the New York Times and whatever other artsy newspapers or magazines they subscribed to... to know it was worth talking to me for long enough, that they could name drop later.

They were nice enough... just a tiny bit too phony for me. I was actually glad when the wife—whose name I had already forgotten—saw someone else she knew and went to say hello.

I turned to speak to my companion, but before I could get one word out, another acquaintance of his was saying hello—and the whole song and dance started over again.

The evening went that way for long enough that I eventually gave up. With each new interruption—he would see someone he knew or someone would recognize me—the subject, and my question, slipped further into the past, at which point it seemed ridiculous to try and bring up the subject now.

I was also beginning to feel quite strange about the fact that I still had no idea what his name was. It felt far too late to ask him something I really should have done before agreeing to go out with him—wine consumption aside. And absolutely no one who recognized him was saying his name. Even the people who recognized me before him seemed to know him—never giving me the chance to hear him tell anyone his name.

The only good news was, a few of the people who recognized me, I knew from the publishing world. None of them were exactly someone I would call a friend, but we saw one other author who published with Hill House. He did not write fantasy, but we had been at several of the same book festivals and parties and were friendly enough. I was also fairly certain he wrote under a pen name, but hadn't felt confident enough to ask him about it.

All in all, aside from not knowing my date's name—and still wondering about his inexplicable reaction to the reporters earlier, the evening was going very well.

It was much the same as every other event like this I had been to. Most of them had been since becoming a well-known author, but there had been a time or two that mom had asked me to go with her to a big charity event in the city.

That first event had been one of the reasons I had chosen a college in New York. Something about the city had captured my heart—and my imagination, and from then on, I could not imagine living anywhere else.

To the entire family's surprise, all three colleges I had applied to in New York accepted me. Choosing one had been one of the most difficult decisions I had ever had to make.

And I had never had a reason to regret choosing the one that had offered me a full scholarship.

With my family lending me zero support in both my chosen profession and my choice of where to attend college, I had needed both the financial support of the school—and the small amount of spare time that had come with being able to work part time to support myself.

When I realized where my thoughts were heading—and the look of concern on my date's face, I shook myself a little and smiled. Years of waitressing and then public appearances had definitely taught me how to smile through even the most difficult things.

I had smiled through migraines at many a personal appearance. I had learned to smile and be personable on zero sleep and after terrifying plane rides... even when I was absolutely starving.

The one difficulty I had was a lack of caffeine. Whether it went hand in hand with a lack of sleep, a deficiency of caffeine intake was nearly impossible to smile through—mostly because I couldn't tell my face muscles what to do when no part of me was awake.

With that thought, I laughed a little. My mysterious date looked over to me with a puzzled expression.

"Did I miss a joke?"

I laughed again. "No. You didn't miss anything. I was just thinking about my caffeine addiction."

"I suppose that means I should be certain they serve you coffee tonight, then."

"Absolutely." I leaned in a little as I smiled up at him. He might be mysterious, but he sure seemed to read me pretty well.

It wasn't long after that unexpected moment when people began to drift out of the large ballroom. I could only imagine they were heading in to the dinner. I found myself hoping this would be one of those events where I would get to sit next to my date—and not across an enormous table from him. He was turning out to be quite an interesting man. Even the whole *not knowing his name* part was working. It was certainly keeping the mystery going.

And yeah, it was more than a little unusual for me.

I was used to dating the sort of guys who wanted something from me, the ones who only saw me as a means to an end—which was probably why I found myself almost never dating.

Well, that, and the amount of time I spend writing.

Most men could not deal with the way writing could take over my life for days at a time. When the words were flowing, I would lock myself away and go with them. And, I had discovered early on that, even though a man wanted to capitalize on my name, he did not want to deal with the schedule or the quirks that went along with it.

The events so far for this evening—along with the intriguing mysteries that surrounded him... and the how and why of his actually asking me to join him tonight... had me wondering which side of that coin he would land on.

We had already met several of his acquaintances and my own here this evening. Not once had he acted like my name was more important than I was. Not once had he preened like a peacock who had caught the prettiest hen.

At least... not yet. Experience had taught me that only time would tell who he was in the end. So, I would have to wait to see the extent of where he stood.

It was a relief to move into the dining room and see that there were round tables set up all around the room. At least I wouldn't have to keep up two conversations with total strangers... and not be able to speak to him for the duration of dinner.

And, I was equally delighted to discover that I actually felt hungry. Evidently, I had shaken off the last of the effects from my bout with food poisoning and the nerves I had felt were completely gone.

I'd been worried that I would have to make a point to pick at dinner—to make it look like I was eating, without actually eating anything.

But now I wouldn't have to worry about that at all.

It did take a few minutes to find our table. Evidently, he'd known the number before we walked into the room. We didn't walk directly to it, but we passed a number of tables before he moved closer to one and walked around until finding our placeholders.

I was not at all surprised when he pulled out my chair and held it for me until I was seated. He had been nothing but a gentleman since I had first met him.

What did surprise me was when I looked to the left of me and saw that there was an author sitting beside me — an all-too familiar name.

Perhaps there would be some drama to come this evening after all.

Initially, when I sat down at the large, round table, and discovered I was seated next to the man who was single-handedly trying to destroy the fantasy world I loved so much, I immediately thought of several things I wanted to say to him. Small jabs that would make him sorry he had ever written anything so mean about the beloved people I had loved for too many years to count.

However, it only took my brain a second to remind me that I wasn't even supposed to know about the manuscript Maria had secretly sent me — much less who had written it.

If I said anything, I could not only get Maria in trouble. I would get her friend in trouble, too. I knew anything I said, even if warranted, could potentially cause many other problems along the way.

So, I'll sit here and say nothing...

When the author looked over at me, I nodded and promptly turned my attention away from him. Maybe ten minutes passed before I heard him talking to the person beside him. When their conversation had continued long enough, I figured I was safe. I turned and looked at the man I desperately wanted to lash out at—but couldn't.

I seethed a little. I studied the man who had stepped into my shoes with his big, messy, war-loving feet, and had effectively killed off everyone and most everything I had loved about the fantastical world I was connected to by more than just words.

He really didn't look all that impressive.

He was just a man, a writer, someone who—like me, had once had a story he wanted to get out into the world. Could I help it if his storyteller mind worked very differently than mine?

Not really.

So, I turned away from him. I talked to my date. I ate the food that was served. I spoke to others around the table, some who knew who I was—you could see it in the way they spoke. A little awed... a bit hesitant... but excited to speak to someone who had written such an amazing story —a story that had captured the imagination and hearts of millions of readers all over the world.

I watched out of the corner of my eye as the man beside me realized who I was.

It was more than a little satisfying to watch a hint of red take over his ears and stain his neck as he clearly connected the dots of who I was and what I had written —and what he had written.

He would be under the same sort of non-disclosure agreement about his work on my series as the other ghost writers. He had to know he couldn't say anything to me or anyone else at the table. He couldn't brag or drop heavy hints about this fabulous work he'd been tapped for.

He just had to sit there and listen to everyone else gush about how much they loved my work and ask questions about what was forthcoming—to see the disappointment, the quiet understanding on their faces as I quoted the standard line that I wasn't allowed to give anything away. They would just have to wait for the publisher to release the news.

And then there was the moment when I saw the tumblers click into place. Something I must have said made him realize that I knew there were ghostwriters taking over further books in the series. I mean, I must know. I knew I wasn't writing them. Something must have made him wonder just how much I knew about who these people were.

He looked over at me with a hesitant smile, a cautious expression that told me he wondered if I knew just who I was sitting next to.

Because, clearly, he had not.

I tried not to give anything away. I tried to school my expression to one of oblivion. To tell him with my face that I knew nothing about the train wreck that was coming.

There was no way to tell if I was successful in my cover. He said nothing. He did nothing. There was no widening of the eyes, no light of discovery, no hints to show whether or not he had put all of the pieces together —just that cautious, polite, business-like smile.

And then the moment was over. He turned away to continue speaking with the person on his other side. And I was left with the feeling that perhaps I had just dodged some sort of bullet.

And then the thought came back to me that he was so much like me —an author with an idea, a story that was clearly as beloved to him as mine was to me.

He could even be going through something just like I

was. Clearly, he had published under his name—or his pen name. There really was no way to know if his backstory was different or just the same as mine. I'd found out the hard way just how cutthroat the publishing world could be. He might have, too. Right this moment, there could be ghostwriters destroying his life's work. I had no way to know.

And I was not about to ask.

I watched him for another moment, an unexpected sympathy and camaraderie for the circumstances and difficulties we both dealt with in this profession that had chosen us welling up within me.

Then I turned back to my date and the people sitting around the table who had so much more they wanted to ask me... say to me.

For about thirty seconds, I sat there listening to the conversation flow around me—before everything sort of dulled out into a strange blur of faces and voices.

I looked out toward the rest of the room and the same thing was happening there as well. The room itself was blurring, the walls turning to smoke and fading into nothing.

The sound blurred and joined to form a strange hum. Then it intensified until I could actually feel it vibrating in my chest... literally pounding in my ears. It took over so absolutely, I couldn't even hear myself breathing. And even then, it kept getting louder... and louder.

It didn't take long for the complete lack of anything concrete to look at, coupled with the intense barrage of sound, to begin making me feel dizzy and a little nauseous. I tried turning my head. I tried shaking my head. I tried covering my ears. Nothing helped. Nothing —not one thing—made even the tiniest difference.

Feeling more than a little desperate, to escape, to get away from whatever was happening around me—to me, I stood. I think I mumbled something about excusing myself, but since I couldn't hear the words, there was no way to be sure.

I started to move away from the table, hoping blindly that I could somehow make my way from the room without knocking anyone down or stumbling over another table.

I never got the chance to take a single step. At the moment I stood, before I had even turned away from the table, everything intensified. The sound that had been blocking out everything before easily became ten times louder—so loud, it felt as if my head might just split open from the intensity. And the strange fog—it turned to such a bright white, it was painful. I tried closing my eyes, but it made no difference. The light was just as intense with my eyes closed as open.

I was literally blind—and, for all intents and purposes, deaf.

And then, just when I was certain I could take no more, it stopped. Everything stopped. There was no sound, no blinding white light—just darkness, as I felt myself swaying, losing my grip on the chair as every single ounce of strength left me and I started to drop.

chapter eighteen

Some people say that even when you're in a coma, you can hear some of what is going on around you. The same could be said of simply losing consciousness. When you start to wake up, it happens in degrees.

First, you hear sounds. They don't make any sense in the beginning. They're all jumbled up in a sort of mob of sound. Or maybe that's more because of how I lost consciousness—due to an overwhelming barrage of sound and light.

Either way, a strange jumble of sound was the first thing I became aware of after blacking out.

As I attempted to think, trying—in my muddled state of mind—to figure out what was going on and where I was. I picked out all sorts of beeps and hums and clicks, an intermittent swooshing sound and a strange hiss. As I listened more intently, almost frightened to try and open my eyes, content to focus on the sounds alone, I realized all of the sounds were independent of each other, not just one mass wave of sound.

It was all still pretty overwhelming, but I comforted myself with the knowledge that at least I was no longer being assaulted with so much intensely loud noise.

Still, it felt like a very long time before I was comfortable enough with what was going on to try and open my eyes.

The moment I did—it's impossible, by the way, to open your eyes just a tiny crack when you've had them closed for a long time... when the muscles are not entirely under your control. The intensity of light that greeted my hesitant vision had me clamping them shut so hard... so fast... in case I was experiencing the same thing that had robbed me of consciousness in the first place.

Thankfully, the light did not invade my closed eyes like it had before. I breathed a sigh of relief. And then took another deep breath to brace myself before opening my eyes again. Thankfully, the muscles responded a little more fully on my second try, opening little by little until I could see that the light was not so bright as I had first feared. It was more the shock of any light to my eyes that have been closed a long time.

Once I was able to open my eyes completely, and see that the light in the room was not that bright at all—in fact, the only true brightness came from a window at the side of the room—I started to look around me, working toward figuring out where I was and how I had gotten there.

It took only seconds to see that I was not in any room of my home. There was absolutely nothing familiar about anything around me, so it clearly was not any of my family's homes either.

There was very little décor around me to give much detail about where I might be. There was a generic sort of chest against the far wall, a large television resting on top of it —two things one would find in any hotel room all over the country. The walls were a nondescript wallpaper, something likely meant to be calming and homey, but mostly just an unattractive color of green.

That little detail was my first clue that I might be in a hospital.

How many times had I heard comments about hospitals

and green? There was no television show that didn't have at least one character who ended up in a hospital at some point during their run. And someone always made a comment about green walls.

Looking around the rest of the room confirmed my suspicions. There was machinery beside my bed which clearly belonged in a hospital, and the bed itself was another clue. I hadn't initially noticed the metal rails that rested on either side of me because they were in the down position instead of raised.

Clearly no one is afraid I'm going to fall out of bed. I guess that's something.

When I turned my head to the other side, to look more closely at the wall with the window, I got my next surprise.

My date... the man whose name I still didn't know... was slumped in a chair beside the bed, a one-use insulated cup on the small table beside him and an open book laying on his lap. His eyes were closed, his head was tilted sideways and slightly forward, and his hair was a tangled mess that looked as if he'd been rolling around on the floor instead of sleeping in a chair.

His suit, the perfectly pressed suit he had been wearing when he arrived to pick me up, was also a mess. His jacket was missing, the shirt was creased and wrinkled and open at the collar. His tie was untied, hanging loosely around his neck, not quite as wrinkled as the shirt. The state of his pants was more difficult to determine, given the book on his lap, the shadows around and underneath that book and the fact that they were black to begin with, but it felt safe to assume they were in the same level of disarray as the rest of his clothing.

A strange warmth spread through me at the sight of him slumped there in what was likely a very uncomfortable chair, asleep and looking as if he'd barely left my side.

It had definitely been worry in his voice at the benefit. It was a strange and slightly troubling revelation for me. What was I supposed to do with this information? And what did that mean for what he might want from me? If he was not like everyone else who wanted to use me as a stepping stone... or a lightning rod, then what exactly did he want?

Was it possible he actually wanted a real relationship?

With me?

He'd gotten my sense of humor. He had even shown he shared some similarities with his own humor. He'd proven he could keep up with me in social circles.

But could he handle the quirks? The long hours writing. Ignoring my phone for days on end. Missing lunch dates or coffee dates because the story sucked me in unexpectedly. How much of that would he put up with before it became too much?

That was the question.

The answer... well, that was anyone's guess—and only time would truly tell. I had also learned that lesson the hard way. I had never thought much about my own patience. I had waited a long time before showing my work to anyone. I'd written and rewritten and rewritten... and rewritten again. Then I'd found Marie and paid her to go over it. Then I'd rewritten it again before I had started sending out queries for an agent.

It had been several months, quite a few rejections, and even more times just being ignored, then one more quick pass with Marie and another rewrite before I had started sending it directly to publishers. There weren't many who even accepted unsolicited manuscripts—and, if I had known what that really meant, I never would have sent the first word to any of them, but I'd been practically desperate at that point.

Looking back, it felt like I'd had both too much and too little patience with the whole situation. There were so many things I would do differently now... with the benefit of knowledge and experience.

Now, if only I had more experience with someone who

actually wanted a relationship with me, instead of just taking what he could get from me and moving on...

There was really no point wishing it true. It wasn't. And I didn't even know if this was what he was thinking. I could sit here what-iffing myself forever and never know the actual answer.

For all I knew, he'd sat there all night out of guilt. He'd taken me to the benefit, and something had happened to me there. He seemed like a real stand up sort of man. He wouldn't just run out on something that he felt like was his fault... obviously.

Now I just had to decide what to do about letting him know I was awake.

I opened my mouth to speak, when the door opened, and in walked a nurse, a doctor—and my agent.

My mouth had been open to speak, but whatever I'd been about to say completely left my brain. So, I shut my mouth—just as the doctor started talking.

"Well. Well. It's about time you woke up, young lady."

When I laughed weakly in answer, he chuckled a little himself, and then continued.

"I'm only half teasing you. Though you have had some people who are quite concerned with your well-being."

He nodded toward the rumpled figure still slumped in the chair on the other side of my bed.

"How are you feeling, Aura? What on Earth happened?" Steve fired off questions to me, but did not give me time to answer before turning his attention to the doctor.

"Doctor, what happened? What caused this? Is she going to be alright now? What can we do to keep this from happening again? Tests... I feel like we should run more tests? The ones you've already done have not given us any answers. Shouldn't we run more? We need answers."

The doctor held up a hand to stop him from going on. Though he did get in one more before finally stopping. "When can she go home?"

The doctor laughed a little. I felt heat creeping up my cheeks a little. Not that I could blame Steve for having so many questions. I had many of the same ones myself. It was his delivery that was a bit overwhelming. He was rushing through the words as if he were somehow in some sort of race to get the questions out first.

"I'll get to all of your questions. I assure you. First, I need to check this young woman out a little."

He turned to the nurse and there must have been some sort of unspoken signal because with very little pressure, it was only a few seconds until she had ushered Steve out of the room and turned back toward the bed.

She shook her head a little as she started toward the end of the bed and continued on around until she was by my head on the other side. I thought I might have seen a little eye roll in there too, but couldn't be sure.

It felt like hours had passed in only these few minutes since the doctor had come in with his nurse and my agent, who was clearly more concerned about the writing I did, than actual concern for me.

Not that I could blame him. My books were making him a lot of money. And there were several projects coming up as well—projects he had been hard at work pitching to the publisher. He wouldn't want to see all that hard work be for nothing.

I just hoped the doctor could give me some sort of explanation for whatever it was that had happened. I turned back toward the doctor to ask what he could tell me... just as he started to speak.

"Well, you can see that I was not joking before. You have had some people very worried about you." He turned a little, looking over his shoulder as he did—and then leaned in a little, his voice low when he went on. "Even if some of them get a little carried away with their concern, it's still always nice to see that my patients have people who care."

I nodded in agreement, not really sure how to answer that since I knew, deep down, it was the books and the money he was concerned about... not really me. But that was apparently enough of an answer for the doctor. He didn't wait for me to say anything.

"Well, I'm certain you have the same questions he just asked... or mostly, anyway."

I nodded again, but didn't interrupt.

"Yes. I thought so. Well..." He flipped over a thick piece of paper or cardboard that had been covering the papers on his clipboard and started scanning down the page, making small little noises as he read certain things, hmms and uh huhs and ahhs. He did that for what felt like a long time before finally flipping the sheet back over the top of his papers and looking back up to me.

"The problem is, there are no problems."

I waited a second for him to say more, but when he didn't, I asked, "No problems? What exactly does that mean?"

"Well, it means that we have run a battery of tests and found absolutely nothing in any of the results that explains why you fainted or why you were unconscious for nearly twenty-four hours after that. We did an EKG. We did a CT scan. We did an MRI. We took x-rays of your head and spine. We did ultrasounds of your heart and lungs. We ran blood work to look for elevated white blood cell counts or low blood sugar. We found absolutely nothing in any of the tests that could have either caused you to faint or to remain unconscious for such an extended period of time."

Again, I waited for him to say more. And again, he didn't.

"But, what does all of that mean?"

He smiled, one of those comforting father-figure type smiles that's intended to make someone feel better. Had I not been an author who had researched that very thing a hundred times, I might have been taken in by it, but I was not. I ignored his smile and listened to the words that came next.

"It means that there is no medical reason for your fainting. Honestly, this is not at all unusual. At least thirty percent of the time someone faints, there's no real medical reason for it. It could be something ridiculously simple, such as an all too common episode known as vasovagal syncope. Fainting can be caused by stimulation of the vagus nerve. It's more common than most people realize and the smallest events can trigger it, resulting in the person fainting."

Here was where I was torn. Did I tell him what had happened? The more I thought about what had happened, the more I had to wonder if it had something to do with my strange alien visitor. And, if that was the case, would anyone believe anything I told them about it —or would it just get me locked up in the psych ward?

"Whatever caused you to lose consciousness, I can assure you that there is nothing causing an ongoing problem. Now, if it happens again, come back. Also, you should make an appointment to follow up with your regular doctor. We'll send over the results we have, even though we didn't find anything."

I was nodding, but murmured an "uh huh" as well. Now that I was thinking along the lines of alien visitors, my mind was coming up with all sorts of crazy theories... theories I did not want to share with anyone.

"Your father..." Here, I did interrupt.

"He's not my father."

The doctor looked back at the door, then back to me — probably wondering more than a little about what had Steve so concerned.

"He's my agent. Literary agent."

"Ahh." was all the doctor said in response.

"Right. He's a worrier." When the doctor still looked unconvinced, I went on.

"There's precedence. I'm not originally from New York and I've gotten myself into worrisome situations before. He's just protective."

Of his investment.

The thought came to me while I was explaining. And I realized as I was defending myself and the relationship I had with my agent, that I really didn't need to worry about what the doctor thought about me.

Perhaps this is one of those worrisome situation Steve tries to protect me from.

"I see. Well, to answer his question about when you can go home, I would like you to stay overnight for observation."

I didn't like the sound of that. I wasn't sure why, but I felt very strongly that I wanted to leave the hospital without being further observed.

"Is that really necessary? I mean, you just said there's really nothing wrong with me—and I've already been here overnight.

"Two nights actually. You were unconscious when they brought you in—and you remained unconscious for nearly forty hours."

That information surprised me. I had thought the benefit

had only been the evening before. Now I was learning it was two nights before. I looked away from the doctor, trying to process that information. Before I could, a noise from beside me drew my attention to the man still occupying the chair beside my bed.

Just as I looked at him, his eyes opened, and he sat up quickly, leaning forward in the chair before standing up and moving to the side of my bed.

"Well, hello there, sleeping beauty," was the first thing he said. And he took my hand in his, gently squeezing my fingers.

I looked down at my hand, surprised at the tingle I felt where our hands touched. Then I looked back up at his face, but he had turned his head to look at the doctor.

"Doctor Reicht, it's good to see you again. What did I miss?"

I looked back over to the doctor, surprised to realize he had already been speaking to the man holding my hand. Then I remembered what he had said about my having been here for two nights already—and it made more sense. They'd been doing tests while I was unconscious. Some of the results would have been back before I woke up. But why would he have shared them with the man beside me?

What exactly had he told the doctors about our relationship that had led them to share confidential medical information with him? What else had happened while I was asleep?

I did not get the chance to ask.

"You haven't really missed much. Results from the last of the tests we conducted came in. The news is good and bad. There is absolutely no medical reason we can find for her fainting."

"Would that be the bad news or the good, then?"

"A little of both actually. We would not be concerned at all if she had simply fainted, and then regained consciousness in a few minutes... or even an hour."

"But she didn't."

"No, she did not. Being unconscious for nearly forty hours concerns me—especially since we can find no medical reason for it. Which is why we would like to keep her at least overnight for observation."

"More tests?" The man beside me prompted, sounding more like a concerned parent than I liked.

"There really are no other tests. We've already run every test we can. Mostly, we want to be sure she isn't going to faint again and stay unconscious for another forty hours

—or longer." The doctor's voice made it sound so reasonable, but if I was at all right about the underlying cause to all of this, they could observe all they wanted and run every test known to man and they wouldn't find a thing.

I didn't say that, of course.

"And... if you do observe her for a day, and she doesn't faint or lose consciousness, you'll just send her home?" There was something odd in his voice, a note of hesitance that had me wondering what he was thinking.

It wasn't like he could possibly know anything I was thinking... could he?

The doctor nodded his head before answering. "That sums it up nicely. There really isn't much more we can do beyond that."

Everyone either sat or stood in silence for a full ten seconds before the doctor cleared his throat—a little obviously. "Well, if there's anything else you need, the nurses will know where to find me. Otherwise, I'll be back to check on you in a few hours."

He looked in my direction and I nodded mutely. There really was no point in arguing. I could never come up with a good enough reason to get them to let me just go home.

"All right then. You're welcome to get out of bed. Walk the halls a bit. I'll just be off to check on my other patients.

And then he was gone—and I was left with a man I barely knew, a man who had witnessed me having a very strange reaction to an alien event.

What was I supposed to do with this? Where was I supposed to go from here?

Before I could figure any of that out, the sound of someone clearing their throat distracted me. I looked up and over to him. He was still standing beside the bed, though he had dropped my hand at some point during the time the doctor had been talking to us.

"Since you're awake... before anyone else comes in, I think there's something I should tell you." His voice was so very serious, I thought surely this would be it. He would tell me it had been a lovely evening, but he had not bargained for any of this. And then he would leave.

I waited, but he said nothing. Understandable. It wasn't an easy thing to say to someone who had just woken up in the hospital after being unconscious for forty hours... after attending an event with him. He probably felt at least a little bit responsible for the situation. Maybe he should.

"This is not an easy thing. Please try not to be angry with me?" His voice was so very soft now. Obviously, he was expecting a scene.

He wouldn't get one. I had been involved in too many crazed book events to cause a scene over something so simple. I would take the news and let it roll off me. He would tell me—and I would be so cool. And then he could go and I would find a way to convince the doctor to let me go home.

"I should have said something before. I really should have. I waited too long. It was just such a fairy tale. I mean, you said yes."

He stopped again—and this time, I was confused. Where was he going with this? It didn't sound precisely like he was about to cut and run. There was something else going on here. But what?

"I know who you are. I mean who you really are. I know everything about you."

"Wait. What?"

END OF BOOK ONE

TO MY READERS

Hello there, and thank you for reading my book!

I wish I could tell you that this is from a true story, but... sadly, I've not been visited by an Alien-like muse of any sort - that I know of, anyway. I wish I knew that, somewhere out there in the cosmos, my stories were somehow supporting a planet full of people.

Oh well. I suppose I will just have to be content with making readers right here on Earth happy.

And, I do hope you're happy with my story. I hope you won't strangle me for leaving you on the knife edge. I promise, I don't do it on purpose. I truly give my characters and their stories complete autonomy - and they tell me when to stop.

I just listen.

THANK YOU!

This one is for all those people out there who believe when there's absolutely zero evidence to back them up!

You know who I'm talking about. And you know what I mean when I say how difficult a position it is to be in. Whether it's faith or aliens or pixies or alternate universes or magical powers, you believe with all that you are.

You devote your mind, your heart, your very soul to a belief that you can't prove, but you feel so strongly is real, that you can't let go of it!

YES! I'm one of you!

I have my wild and crazy theories that almost no one else shares. I believe in things I have zero evidence for, other than how strongly I feel that it is real—whether anyone believes with me or not.

Thank you for reading! Thank you for holding on! Thank you for believing!

Blessed be!

Siren's Charm
CALL OF THE SEA · BOOK ONE
AVERY SAGE

TURN THE PAGE

for a sneak peek at Avery's
recently released:
Siren's Charm

chapter one

LOOKING DOWN AT MY PHONE AS I WALKED through the store, I purposely slowed my steps as I answered the message that appeared.

"Let me know when you get there."

Then, before I could type more than a word. . .

"Be sure to check on all three."

"And ask about any sort of deals they have going."

"Find out if they match prices."

My breath whooshed out as I typed as fast as possible on the tiny little screen, trying to answer all of the questions quickly, so I could get the errand over with and get to my favorite coffee place. *"I'm almost there. I will. Yes. OK."*

I desperately need caffeine.

Hitting the send button, with another sigh, I stepped forward again—and bumped solidly into someone. When I looked up at him, it was easy to see that he had been standing right in front of me the whole time. I just hadn't seen him. Embarrassment sent heat rushing into my cheeks, likely turning them a bright shade of red.

Oh my word. How did I miss seeing him there?

Even as the thought came to me, I knew the answer. I had been staring at my stupid phone.

Feeling ridiculous, fumbling in my mind for some way to apologize, I just stood there, staring up at him. It was difficult to look away. Especially since he was well over six feet tall, broad-shouldered, and clearly well-muscled, since bumping into him had felt like ramming into a wall.

And standing there. . . just looking at him, the strangest thing happened. I completely and totally lost track of time. I mean, it could have been an hour—or a second—but there was literally no way to know how long I stood there, just staring at him.

At some point, the heat of embarrassment changed into a very different type of heat. Everything about him, from his dark, wavy hair to his tall, muscular physique, to his well tailored clothes, told me this man was about as far out of my league as you could get.

At that point, I forcibly stopped myself from staring. I made myself look down, finally finding my voice and mumbling something that I dearly hoped sounded like an apology.

"Not at all, Miss. Please excuse me." The deep, masculine voice sent a little shiver along my skin, almost as if the man had brushed a kiss along my neck instead of the whisper of breath that had reached me with his words.

"Oh, no. . . I. . ." I made the mistake of looking up at him again and words failed me. It was not something I was accustomed to—having been teased my entire life about my ability to strike up a conversation with a perfect stranger and know their entire life story in the course of a long line waiting to order coffee. But no words came now. Not to me, anyway.

"Are you all right?" Again, his voice sent a little shiver along my skin and I could only nod, struck completely dumb by my disorienting reaction to him.

"Are you certain?" He asked the question as his eyes searched my face and beyond—presumably for outward signs of an injury.

When he took my hand a moment later and led me over to where mattresses were lined up side by side in long rows, the heat that had started to build in my midsection spread to my arm. . . and every square inch in between. Everywhere his hand touched mine, it felt as if it were aflame and I began to wonder if I had done some sort of damage, though I didn't remember hitting my head—and surely that was the only thing that would account for such confusion and ridiculous behavior.

"I. . ." None of the words I wanted to say would form on my tongue, and I shook my head in an attempt to clear it.

My phone chose that moment to vibrate, and when he dropped my hand, the fuzzy thoughts in my head started to clear a bit. I looked down at my mother's message with a sense of relief.

She might have been annoying me before, but she was saving me now—and I would not forget it anytime soon.

"Are you there yet?"

I typed in a quick reply, *"Yes. I just got here."* Then I took a deep breath, almost hoping that when I looked up again, the strange and oddly compelling man would be gone. But he was still standing beside me, looking down at my phone with a very odd expression on his handsome features.

Now the words came, flooding out and tumbling over each other on their rush out of my mouth.

"Sorry. She's just really concerned over this mattress. She saw they were on sale, and I just happened to be out, so she sent me to check out the situation. It's been way too long since we replaced ours, so we really need new ones." The moment the words left my mouth, I realized what I had just said to this stranger who I had essentially run into only moments before—and the heat rushed back to my cheeks.

Fortunately, he was either a gentleman or somehow he hadn't picked up on my major faux-pas. "Well, I suppose I should let you get on with it, then." He stepped back a little, then stopped. "If you're certain you are all right. . . ."

"I am. Thank you." He nodded and moved away then. I stayed right where I was for a few more seconds, desperately trying to slow my erratic heartbeat.

When I stood, I walked aimlessly around the area, trying

to make it look as if I were shopping, but nothing I was looking at made any sense to my muddled brain. There were too many thoughts rushing around to make any sense of even one of them. Nothing made sense in my head. My reaction to him had been completely unexpected and intense in a way I was not used to.

There was still a ridiculous amount of heat in my cheeks, my arm, my chest. There was also a tingle lingering on my skin where he had touched me. My breathing had not yet returned to normal and for some strange reason, I felt a strong urge to giggle.

This is ridiculous. I told myself. Why am I feeling like a teenager, a silly teenager at that?

I had never really been one to giggle over boys and make a fool of myself, so my behavior felt doubly odd. Clearly, it had been too long since I had been around a handsome man.

And he certainly was that. *I don't know when I've met a more handsome man.*

My blood felt as if it was rushing everywhere. My heartbeat was still erratic. My breaths were still coming a little too fast. When had a good looking man ever affected me this way?

Since I couldn't think of a time, I decided to go back to

the idea that I had somehow smacked my head—either when I'd bumped into him or just after.

Maybe on a shelf when I stumbled backwards—and that's why everything still feels a little confused and muddled in my head...

Indeed, it did. The more I tried to focus on what exactly had happened when I'd bumped into him, the less clear it was in my head.

So I stopped trying.

The notification sound from my phone reminded me what I was supposed to be doing. I shook myself a little and tried to focus on the task at hand; finding those mattresses. Looking around me, still trying to clear the confusion in my head, I realized I had stopped in front of one of the three mattresses Mom had actually sent me to look at. Laughing at myself a little now—I mean, just how ridiculous is this day going to get—I tried to focus, to really look at the information on the sign next to it.

Everything was just like I had expected it to be, which was good since I was still feeling a little loopy and silly. Using my phone, I took a picture of the sign, glad to have the easy out, before looking around again to see if I could spot one of the others.

When I left the store, I intended to drive straight to my favorite coffee shop. However, my head still felt like it was spinning, and I took two wrong turns before actually arriving there.

Once I did, I sat in my car for nearly a minute, still trying to get my heart to calm down. Just the tiniest thought of the man I'd encountered would send it racing, dragging my breath with it, leaving me feeling loopy and light-headed and almost as if I weren't even touching the ground around me.

Caffeine. That's what I need. Something to wake me up, snap me out of this.

Squaring my shoulders, I stepped out of the car, closed the door, turned toward the store, and nearly tripped over my own feet.

Standing there, right by the door, was the same man I was trying desperately to get out of my head. *Why? Why is he here? How is that fair?*

I tried twice to open my mouth and make some sort of flippant remark about what a small world it was or something to the tune of maybe he was following me, but both times the words failed me. They got all jumbled up in my head when I started to say them, and I ended up closing my mouth again.

He didn't move until I got close to the door. I couldn't tell if he was simply being a gentleman, waiting to open the door for me or if he was actually waiting for me. I moved slowly, doing my best to keep any part of my body from touching him.

I did not want or need my brain getting jumbled again, and some part of me was absolutely certain it would if I even brushed up against him. Fortunately, I made it through the door and into the coffee shop without touching any part of him. However, he walked through the doorway right behind me, so closely that I could almost swear that I could feel heat from his body.

I made my way to the line. He followed me all the way. I stepped up behind an older lady who looked as if she had no idea what she wanted or how to figure it out.

Normally, I would have struck up a conversation with her, made a joke or a silly comment about how many choices they gave us, but I was having more difficulty than I wanted to admit making sense of the menu myself. I often made a point of trying new things, but I couldn't seem to decide what I was in the mood for.

Fortunately, the barista behind the counter recognized me when I stepped up. "Your usual today or are you trying something new?"

I looked up at the menu again, still trying to make sense of it, but after a few seconds, I knew it was hopeless so I caved. "Make it the usual."

"The usual it is, then. And I'm going to add a shot of coffee. You look like you need it today." She spoke quietly, but I could see concern in her eyes.

She knew me pretty well, had seen me on some of my craziest days—the sort of days I would joke about needing my coffee in an IV drip. If she thought I looked out of it, I must be worse off than even I was thinking.

Unsure of what to say—and more than a little worried about what might come out, especially with the handsome stranger still right behind me—I nodded my head, waved my phone over the little sensor to pay and then moved away.

When I stepped to the side, I did not anticipate the distance well enough, or else he had moved closer to me. I bumped solidly into him again and every thought in my head turned to mush—again.

All I could do was stand there and feel... first, the heat that felt as if it were pouring out of him and into me, then the confusion as my thoughts scattered every which way in my head. The heat of embarrassment again filling my cheeks. And there was a strange feeling underneath it all, something that I couldn't quite latch onto—even though it felt as if it were pulling at me, dragging at me, trying to move my whole being somehow.

It almost felt as if he were trying to communicate with me, as if there was a tiny little voice inside, telling me something... but what, I had no idea.

And suddenly the heat cooled just a little. It didn't disappear entirely, but it did give me enough room in my head to step away. Nearly everything within me wanted to turn and look at him again as I moved away, but the tiniest part of me knew that would be a very bad idea—and though, it was likely the most difficult thing I had ever done, I slowly walked over to where I would pick up my coffee.

Not more than a minute later, he walked up beside me, obviously waiting as well. It took every ounce of self control I could get hold of to keep myself from looking up at him. We stood there for about a minute before my name was called. I picked up my drink and turned away from the counter as quickly as possible, nearly colliding with a young woman who had come up behind me to wait for her own order.

Once I sidestepped her, I rushed toward the door. I nearly turned back around when I saw that he was standing right there, waiting to open it for me again. It was several seconds before I could get my feet to move.

He just stood there, with a sort of half smile on his ridiculously handsome features, waiting — for me, obviously.

I was careful again to avoid touching or brushing against him, but the heat I'd felt before was there, almost as if it were reaching out to me and I could feel my breathing speed up. My heart started pounding, and my thoughts scattered again.

What is wrong with me? What is it about this man? Why can't I seem to shake this off?

But there was no answer — none at all. I pushed myself to move quickly through the doorway and head for my car, not daring to look back at him or see which direction he went.

I should have... and I would have... if only I could have.

But again my thoughts were muddled. About two seconds after I shut my door, I turned to set down my coffee, and let out a yelp when I saw him sitting in my passenger seat.

"What are you doing!?" I half yelled, half whispered the question, worried first that I might elicit some strange reaction in him, second that someone outside the car might see or hear me and get a very wrong impression of what was going on.

"I'm here for you." That deep, masculine, slightly husky voice danced along every nerve in my body again, sending chills and shivers up and down my spine even while visions of dark rooms and late nights, steamy encounters and passionate embraces filled my head.

He wasn't touching any part of me, but my body felt as if he were running his hands all over me. It was a sensation I was not accustomed to. I wanted to demand he get out of my car. I wanted to ask him what he meant. I wanted to move across the seat and climb into his lap.

The last thought shocked me more than a little. Where had that come from? I didn't think things like that — normally. It must be something he was doing. Was there some control he had over me that I was not aware of? There was no other explanation that made a bit of sense. As if any of the things that had happened since the moment I had first bumped into this strange man made even a tiny amount of sense.

Just when panic started to take hold of me, I told myself to lean back, take a deep breath, then look at him with some sort of detachment. However, he didn't give me the chance. He leaned forward, slid a hand into my hair and covered my lips with his.

The heat that had been running through me ever since I'd first collided with him exploded when his lips touched mine. Every thought I'd started to collect, every question, every fear, every worry... every one of them scattered into tiny little shards of nothing and I felt myself lean into the kiss, unexpectedly hungry for more.

All on its own, my hand moved up his jacket and wrapped around his neck. I tilted my head a little as his lips moved over mine. That same heat wrapped itself in little tendrils around every part of me until I felt like I was a flame being consumed by an unexplainable force that held me to him like a lifeline.

His other hand moved around to my back, pulling me even closer to him while he deepened the kiss. My mouth opened on a little moan as his lips moved away from my mouth, but any complaint I might have had drifted away as his lips scorched a path down my neck and across my collarbone.

He said something against my skin, but nothing registered in my brain outside of the heat and passion crashing over me in strong, intense waves. I tried to pay attention when he spoke again, but nothing he was saying made a bit of sense. I shook my head a little when he pulled away and looked at me with a somewhat odd expression on his face.

And then those waves crashing over me felt real. Suddenly I was cold—icy cold. In shock, I sputtered, trying to wiggle out of his grip, to move away from him, to catch my breath in the suffocating vortex of cold that was pulling me under.

And then everything went black.

ABOUT THE AUTHOR

Avery Sage started her career under a different pen name, under a different impression about who she was as a person, and under what she thought was a ticking time clock...

Avery writes fantastical stories about people who are surprised by love, people who find themselves in unreal situations, people who go off on exciting adventures and people who find their way through thrilling escapades!

Avery is an active part of the LGBTQIA community who enjoys writing the sort of stories you won't find just anywhere, filled with the sorts of characters you won't find between the pages of just any book.

Follow Avery on her journey through writing, editing, more editing, procrastinating, even more editing . . .

ABOUT THE PUBLISHER

Otherworldly Press publishes inclusive fantasy, romantasy and urban fantasy with an emphasis on lgbtqia+ characters for both adult and young adult readers.

We pride ourselves on offering the type of stories that readers can disappear into when the world around us gets to be a little too real. . .

Escape in our fantasy! Slip into our romantasy! Adventure with our urban fantasy!

As long as you READ!